CHRISTMAS CANDLES

Two Holiday Novellas

MARY JO PUTNEY

PANDAMAX
PRESS

CONTENTS

INTRODUCTION

I'VE WRITTEN QUITE a lot of novellas, but they've been scattered through many years and multiple publishers. Luckily, independent publishing makes it possible to collect shorter works so they're readily available for interested readers. Christmas collections are particularly nice around the holidays when we're all busy, time is short, but we need a "happily ever after" fix!

The Best Husband Money Can Buy was originally published in an anthology called *A Stockingful of Joy*. The story was inspired by a short filler article in the *Baltimore Sun* that I'd read a number of years earlier. The article told of a Spanish businessman who happened to stop into a church while visiting Stockholm, Sweden. The church was empty except for a coffin. The Spaniard, a devout Catholic, knelt and prayed for twenty minutes or so, then signed a condolence book that asked for the names of anyone who prayed for the deceased. No one else had signed.

After returning home, he received a call from Stockholm announcing that he would inherit the entire fortune of the man who had died, a successful real estate dealer who had left no close relatives. The Spanish gentleman's generous act of faith had made him a millionaire, and provided me with an irresistible hook for a story.

Years later, I read that this story was apocryphal, though it was picked up by many newspapers. But the inspiration it provided for *The Best Husband Money Can Buy* was quite real! I hope you enjoy reading about Emma and Anthony and how their marriage of convenience becomes a true love match.

Mad, Bad, and Dangerous To Know was originally written for a Signet "bad boy" anthology called *Rakes and Rogues,* and the title is from a famous quote Lady Caroline Lamb made about her lover, Lord Byron. It's the only Western novella I've ever written, and I think the setting was inspired by the first sentence which floated into my mind from somewhere. Then I had to figure out a story to go with that beginning!

Though *Mad, Bad* wasn't originally written as a holiday story, when I was looking for a first-time-in-digital novella to pair with *The Best Husband Money Can Buy*, I realized that my Western tale was well suited to a Christmas setting. Plus I love writing holiday stories, and this gave me a chance to do more Christmas. I also love the image of candles in the windows welcoming travelers to the warmth of a home.

I hope you enjoy this story of two despairing and lonely people who are drawn together by chance, and who find so much more than they ever dreamed possible.

Happy holidays!
Mary Jo

THE BEST HUSBAND MONEY CAN BUY

CHAPTER 1

IT WAS Emma Stone's annual day for sadness.

She returned to her room after an exhausting session of trying to drum manners and mathematics into her charges, and found a letter waiting for her. The heavy, expensive paper and Vaughn seal were instantly recognizable, as was the exquisite script that said "Miss Emma Vaughn Stone."

She picked the letter up with a sigh, not yet ready to open it. There was no need to, really. Inside, in the handwriting of the Duchess of Warrington's secretary, would be an invitation to the annual Vaughn Christmas gathering at Harley, the family seat. Two weeks of talk and laughter and celebration among dozens of Vaughns of varying degree, with the duke and duchess presiding over the festivities.

Nostalgically she thought back to happier days when she'd attended every year. Troops of young cousins galloping through the house and grounds. Older Vaughns fondly remembering their shared past. Feasts that made the tables groan. The candlelit Christmas Eve service in the castle chapel. She could almost smell the roasting chestnuts...

Face set, she broke the seal and looked inside. The invitation was exactly like all the others, even though it had been over ten years since she had attended one of the gatherings. Ten long years, since her parents had died and left Emma impoverished.

Her mother had been a second cousin of the duke, and every year she had brought her husband and daughter for Christmas. Emma wondered how much longer it would be until she was dropped from the list. Even if she could take a fortnight off from her governess position, she would not go to Harley. She was too poor, too insignificant, to belong in that gilded world anymore.

It hurt to receive the invitation every year and know that she could not attend. It would hurt even more when the Warringtons finally stopped inviting her. The annual invitation was her last fragile connection to her happy childhood.

Unbearably restless, Emma caught up her cloak so that she could walk through the London streets. For the next few hours, she'd think of the past, a self-indulgence she allowed herself only once a year. By the time she returned to the Garfields' house, she would be tired enough to sleep, if she was lucky.

Giving silent thanks for the fact that it was her half-day off, she went out into the raw December afternoon. As her long strides carried her east along the Strand, she thought of those distant golden holidays, and wondered what had happened to her grand relations. There was quiet young Lord Brandon, known as Brand, who was son and heir to the duke. He had two younger sisters within a few years' age of Emma. And Cecilia, who like Emma was a distant cousin Unlike Emma, she was wealthy and beautiful.

And, of course, there was Anthony Vaughn, Brand's best friend, another distant cousin who would someday be Viscount Verlaine. Five years older than Emma, Anthony had been the leader of the younger generation, outrageously handsome, and sometimes merely outrageous, but so charming that everyone always forgave him. On her last Christmas at Harley, it had been obvious that he and Cecilia were heading for a match. They'd made a stunningly attractive couple. Emma had come across them kissing in a corner once. She'd made an embarrassed retreat, unnoticed by the young lovers.

She had usually gone unnoticed, being plain and shy, but she didn't mind that. What mattered was that she had belonged.

Emma detoured to the Covent Garden market to buy herself a nosegay of flowers. It was an expensive luxury at this season, but one that she permitted herself now and then. To always watch every penny was bad for the soul. She loved flowers, and this small bunch of chrysanthemums would brighten her drab room for days.

She continued eastward into the old City of London, the financial and merchant district, until a glance at the gray sky showed that it was time to turn back. Though

Emma felt safe enough on these streets in daylight, she wanted to be home by dark.

On impulse, she decided to visit the church on the corner. Like most of the parish churches in the City, it was suffering as residents moved farther from London's center. Still, the church was handsome, and it would be a welcome respite from the cold wind.

Inside, she sat for a few minutes and gave a prayer for her parents. They had died of a fever when Emma was at school in Bath. That terrible shock had been followed by another when she returned home to find that after the debts were paid, there would be no money left. Her amiable father had inherited a modest independence and spent every penny of it, along with his wife's marriage portion. There would be no income or dowry for his daughter.

The day after Emma's parents had been buried, a letter came from the Dowager Duchess of Warrington. In crisp, formal words, she offered the orphan a home at Harley. Even at fifteen, Emma had known what that meant—a lifetime as a poor relation, entitled to room and board in return for performing menial services for the duchess and other members of the household.

If she'd been pretty, she might have accepted. Many people came to Harley, and there might have been a man willing to marry an attractive girl with no dowry.

But Emma was tall and robust and unremarkable, with dark hair and freckles and eyes of shifting color that never stayed the same long enough to be called gray or green or hazel. If she'd gone to Harley, she would have spent the rest of her life—decades, probably—as an unpaid servant. Inevitably, she would be known as Poor Emma. That is, if she were noticed at all.

Luckily, there had been another choice. The headmistress of Emma's school offered to let her stay and complete her education in return for helping with the younger students. At eighteen, Emma was made a full-fledged teacher.

She enjoyed teaching, so when the headmistress retired and sold the school, Emma became a governess. Usually governesses were older, but it was one profession where plainness was an asset. She'd spent several years with the family of a prosperous doctor. When the daughters no longer needed her, she'd taken her current position with the Garfields.

The Garfields. Emma sighed at the thought as she got to her feet and began to stroll around the church. There was much carved wood, and several fine funeral brasses.

She was almost ready to leave when she noticed a coffin lying in a side chapel. The pine box looked very stark, with no mourners or flowers or even any candles lit. Tucked in the corner where the rail met the wall was a book open to show blank pages. Curiously she looked closer, and saw a note asking those who prayed for the deceased to leave their name and address.

A HARRIED CURATE emerged from the vestry and walked

down the aisle past her. Hesitantly Emma said, "Excuse me, sir. Who was this man?"

The clergyman paused. "Though Harold Greaves was a member of this congregation, he seldom came to services, so I know very little about him. He was seventy years old. Died of an apoplexy, I believe. He'll be buried tomorrow."

"He had no family?"

"Apparently not." With a nod, the curate continued on his way.

Emma stared at the empty condolence book. It seemed unbearably sad that a man should have lived so many years and left no one to mourn.

For a moment she wondered who would mourn her death. Then, ashamed of the self-pity she'd been indulging in since receiving the invitation to Harley, she knelt beside the coffin and prayed for the soul of Harold Greaves.

As she did, she imagined him as a small child. Since no infant survived without being fed and washed and tended, there must have been someone who cherished him then. In his seventy years, surely he had made friends. She prayed that he had known his share of happiness and satisfaction, and that his death had been a swift and easy one.

Gradually a sense of peace came over her. She hoped that meant Mr. Greaves was resting easy. A little stiff from the cold stone floor, she got to her feet. After a moment of struggle with her own selfish impulses, she laid her nosegay on the coffin. For her, there would be other flowers, but not for Harold Greaves. May his soul rest in peace.

Not wanting to leave the pages of the condolence book so desolately blank, she used the pencil lying in the middle to write her name and the address of the Garfields' house. After a moment's thought, she also printed out the words of the Twenty-Third Psalm. *Yea, though I walk through the valley of the shadow of death, I will fear no evil, for Thou art with me....*

After she finished the psalm, she left the church, walking hastily, for it was almost dark. But the sense of peace stayed with her. It was true that she did not have the comfortable life with husband and family that she had grown up expecting, but she was alive and healthy and she'd never gone hungry.

Counting her blessings, she hurried home.

FIVE DAYS after Emma received the invitation to Harley, a footman interrupted her French lesson with the two Garfield daughters. "The mistress wants you to come downstairs," he said slyly. "You have a caller."

"For me? How odd." Wondering who could possibly want to see her, Emma got to her feet. "Letty, Isabelle, work on your translations until I return."

Letty rolled her eyes elaborately while her younger sister giggled. The two girls were unrewarding students, interested only in clothing and endless speculations about the men they would someday marry. They were also idle and spoiled by their mother. Emma hoped that in time she would be able to inspire them with some respect for learning, but she wasn't optimistic.

"Maybe Miss Stone has a gentleman caller," Isabelle whispered.

Letty sniffed. "An old thing like her? Hardly."

Emma didn't know if she was supposed to hear the interchange or not, so she decided to ignore it. Still, her color was high when she went downstairs.

Mrs. Garfield was seated in the drawing room with a silver-haired gentleman on the chair opposite. As he got his feet, she said with obvious disapproval, "Mr. Evans insists that he must speak with you privately about a most important matter." Her eyes narrowed to slits. "I'll have no goings on in my house, miss."

Mr. Evans said in a formidably well-bred voice, "I assure you, Mrs. Garfield, my business with Miss Stone is entirely professional." His tone was enough to rouse Mrs. Garfield and send her from the room. Then he turned to Emma.

"Sir, are we acquainted?" she asked, her brow furrowed. "If so, I'm afraid that I have forgotten the circumstances."

He smiled and looked much more approachable. "We are not acquainted, Miss Stone. I am a solicitor with news I think you will welcome. Please, do sit down. This will take some time."

Welcome news? As Emma settled on the sofa, she tried to think of any aged relations who might have left her a legacy, but without success. The rich Vaughns all had closer kin to leave their money to.

The solicitor resumed his seat. "First, are you the Emma Stone who five days ago left your name in the condolence book of Mr. Harold Greaves at the church of St. Giles-without-Cripplegate in the City of London?"

Startled, she said, "Yes. I'm sorry, I meant no harm. Is there some family member who was offended by a stranger praying for Mr. Greaves?"

"Quite the contrary. Mr. Greaves was a widower. He and his wife had no children, and there are no other close kin." Mr. Evans paused, his eyes distant. "He and his wife were very close. After she died several years ago, Harold became something of a recluse. They were both good friends of mine as well as clients."

"I'm sorry for your loss," Emma said politely. She managed, barely, not to ask what this had to do with her.

"My friend left a most unusual last will and testament. He said that because he had no surviving family, anyone who freely prayed for his soul would receive 'the sum total of his worldly goods.'" The solicitor smiled. "You were the only one to sign the condolence book. Therefore, Miss Stone, you are the sole heir of Harold Greaves, merchant of London."

"Simply for spending a quarter of an hour in prayer?" Emma said incredulously.

"It was a quarter hour that no one else spent," Mr. Evans pointed out. "Harold always had a great appreciation for disinterested goodness. He would be happy to know that you prayed for no other reason than the simple caring of a good heart."

Emma held very still, trying to absorb the solicitor's announcement. Merely because she had chanced to wander into that small church, then spent a few minutes praying, she was now an heiress. She wondered how much Mr. Greaves had left. It would be a great blessing to have several hundred pounds as a cushion against unemployment or illness. Even fifty pounds would be very welcome.

Mr. Evans said jovially, "Aren't you going to ask how much you will inherit?"

Emma colored. "I'm curious, of course, but it seems rather vulgar to ask. I assume that you wouldn't be here unless there was some amount left after paying Mr. Greaves' funeral expenses."

"There is indeed." Mr. Evans paused portentously. "It's too soon to give an exact figure, but it is safe to say that your inheritance will be about one hundred thousand pounds."

Emma's jaw dropped. Sure she had not heard correctly, she repeated, "You said...one hundred pounds?"

The solicitor chuckled. "You didn't mishear. The estate is approximately one hundred thousand pounds. You are now a very wealthy young woman, Miss Stone."

There was a roaring in Emma's ears and for a moment she thought she would faint. A hundred thousand pounds! The daughter of the richest banker in Britain had gone to her noble husband with a dowry of one hundred thousand pounds. It was a fortune that would not disgrace the daughter of a duke.

Could this be some kind of dreadful joke at her expense? Her gaze went to the solicitor's face. Sober, respectable, patently honest. Exactly the kind of solicitor that a rich merchant would have. She tried to clear her throat, but her voice still came out as a squeak. "Excuse me, sir. I...I'm having trouble taking this in."

"Naturally. Strokes of fortune such as this are life-changing." He cocked his head to one side. "Do you have any idea what you will do with your inheritance?"

The question focused Emma's churning thoughts. "I wish to tithe a tenth of the amount to charity. For the widows and children of our gallant soldiers who died fighting Napoleon, I think."

"Very proper," Mr. Evans said approvingly. "What else?"

Emma could travel to Italy and Greece and all those wonderful, exotic places that were no more than names on the map. Buy a house, or an estate. Do a thousand things.

Did she want to do them alone? She realized with shock that she had just been given the chance to obtain the most powerful desire of her heart—a home and family of her own. She could once more have a place where she belonged.

Struggling to control her excitement, Emma said, "I'm going to get myself a husband, Mr. Evans. The best husband money can buy."

CHAPTER 2

THE SOLICITOR BLINKED at Emma's bald announcement. Then he gave her an unprofessional grin. "You're a very direct young lady, Miss Stone. What sort of husband would that be?"

"I'm not that young, Mr. Evans, but I am practical and not at all romantic." At least, not in the last ten years. Once Emma had been as romantic as any young girl. A man's face appeared in her mind. Ruthlessly she suppressed the image. "I want someone of good character who will treat me with kindness and respect. Well-bred. Pleasing to look at, but he needn't be handsome. If fact, it would be much better if he is not."

If a handsome man married a plain woman, everyone would think it was only for money. Emma did not want that to be said of her, even if it was true.

The solicitor gave an approving nod. "In other words, what any wise woman would want in a husband. But you mentioned 'well-bred.' Did you mean a titled aristocrat?"

He hesitated, then said with some awkwardness, "Forgive me, but men of that class can be...difficult. There are those who would happily take your money while despising you for being of lower birth."

She raised her chin. "My mother was a Vaughn. No man would dare look down on my birth."

"You are one of the Vaughns of Harley?" Mr. Evans's raised brows were a surprised comment on her status as a little more than an upper servant.

"The relationship is close enough that I am invited to the castle on great occasions," she said dryly, "but not close enough for me to have any money."

As she spoke, Emma suddenly realized that she could accept the Christmas invitation to Harley. That prospect was far more vivid and compelling than the abstract knowledge that she had just inherited a fortune. She could return to the scene of her happiest days, a Vaughn once more. She wanted to laugh aloud with joy.

The solicitor's tone changed from avuncular interest to crisp professionalism. "No matter whom you marry, I suggest that you allow me or another competent solicitor to set up a special trust so that, say, half of your capital is reserved to you and your children. Normally a woman's property becomes her husband's when she marries, but a woman of great wealth, such as you are now, often prefers to keep some control in her own hands."

She was now a woman of great wealth. Emma wanted to laugh again, this time in disbelief. "An excellent idea. I've seen women ruined by profligate husbands." She bit her lip. "I have no idea how to manage so much money. Will you act for me, as you did for Mr. Greaves?"

"It would be my honor, and my pleasure," the solicitor said promptly.

"I shall need rather a lot of help, and not only financial." She smiled with wry self-mockery. "Would you be able to use your connections to compile a list of possible husbands? Men who fit the requirements I mentioned earlier, and whose circumstances compel them to seek a rich wife. In other words, the better grade of fortune hunter."

Mr. Evans regarded her with fascination and a certain shock. "As I said, you are…admirably direct. I shall make inquiries among my legal colleagues about suitable candidates. Character will be of the utmost importance in these circumstances."

His eyes narrowed thoughtfully. "I can think of several men who might suit. There's the Honorable George Martin, a widower with four fine children. An admirable fellow. Or Sir Edward Wyckham, a rising young politician. He has great ability, but he'll need a wife of means to make the most of his opportunities." The solicitor smiled dismissively. "We wouldn't want you to pledge yourself to a charming wastrel such as young Lord Verlaine."

"Verlaine?" She caught her breath. "If the current viscount is a young man, I presume that means the second viscount has died and his son Anthony has inherited."

"Yes. Sorry, I forgot that Verlaine is a Vaughn," Mr. Evans said, expression stricken. "He is related to you?"

"A distant cousin," Emma said, her heart pounding. "I remember him from Christmases at Harley. I'm fearfully out of touch with the family. I thought that he'd married another of my cousins. Or is he a widower?"

"As far as I know, Verlaine has never been married. Certainly he is single now." The solicitor frowned. "If you know him, you'll also know how unsuitable he would be. Too handsome, too charming, and thoroughly unreliable. His name is a byword for every kind of wild prank, and they say he gambles heavily. I know for a fact that his estate is on the brink of foreclosure."

Anthony. Single and in need of a rich wife. "I agree that he is probably inappropriate. Still, Verlaine has the advantage of being known to me." She rubbed her damp palms on her skirt. "Please look into his circumstances. If it appears that he would be interested in the kind of... arrangement I propose, he might be worth considering."

"As you wish," the solicitor said without enthusiasm. "But I will be able to present much better prospects."

"I'm sure you can," Emma said, pleased with her calm tone.

Yet after she and the solicitor concluded their business and he took his leave, she leaned back in her chair, her cold hands locked together. A fortune, Christmas at Harley—and Anthony. Granted, he'd always been a bit wild, but there had been no real vice in him. In his casual way, he'd been kind to her. If he really needed money enough to be willing to marry for it...

She tried to control her turbulent thoughts, but without success. She wanted to buy herself a husband. If so, why not Anthony Vaughn if he was willing?

Anthony, the only man she had ever loved.

EVENTS MOVED QUICKLY after Mr. Evans left. Full of curiosity and bad temper, Mrs. Garfield had immediately confronted Emma about the purpose of the solicitor's visit. Since Emma no longer had to tolerate her employer's rudeness, she promptly quit her position, effective in one week.

Another governess was found. Emma silently wished her well with the Garfield daughters. Then, because she needed a maid to be considered respectable, she hired away one of Mrs. Garfield's housemaids. Becky was a pleasant, quiet young woman who was bullied unmercifully by the housekeeper because she could read and write and wanted to better herself. She accepted Emma's offer to be a lady's maid with relief and enthusiasm.

The day after Emma and her new maid took up residence in the very expensive and fashionable Grillon's Hotel, a sheaf of papers arrived from the solicitor. Each page listed a prospective husband. With amusement, Emma noticed how Mr. Evans had done his best to make each sound appealing. One man had "a bright, engaging manner," while another was "owner of a splendid Yorkshire estate, only moderately mortgaged."

She paged through the pile impatiently. The very last

was "Anthony Vaughn, third Viscount Verlaine." No enticing descriptions for him, only comments like, "His estate, Canfield, is on the brink of foreclosure." "Gambles heavily" came with the grudging note, "Usually wins, though he has never been publicly accused of cheating."

Emma smiled at that. Unless Anthony had changed beyond recognition, he would never cheat.

Then she lowered the paper, her expression sobering. She was a fool, of course. She had never really known Anthony well. The last time she'd seen him, he had been a man grown while she was still a girl in the schoolroom. She'd spun dreams around him, cherished his occasional friendly words, and loved him with the innocent fervor of a very young girl. In another year or so, she would surely have outgrown her infatuation if she had continued in her old life.

But everything had changed irrevocably when she was fifteen, and she had never had a real chance for romance. The closest she had come was when a drunken guest at her former employer's had cornered her for a kiss. It had not been an enjoyable experience. No wonder her old dreams about Anthony had stayed alive in her heart.

She glanced back at the dossier, and realized that Anthony had rooms on Bruton Street, literally around the corner from Grillon's Hotel. It wouldn't hurt to walk by. In fact, it might be a good idea to call on him. As his cousin, it wouldn't be too improper for her to do so. A single short visit should be enough for her to strike him from the list of prospects. Then she would be free of her childish dreams, and able to put him from her mind forever.

Quickly, before she could become frightened by her own temerity, she donned her coat and went off to call on her cousin.

Her resolve faltered when she reached the building where Anthony lived. It contained several sets of rooms for gentlemen, with Anthony's flat on an upper floor. She stared at the plain facade, wondering if she dared enter. It wasn't too late to turn back, and doing so would probably save her great humiliation.

But she had to know. Jaw set, she went up the steps and into the common hallway. There was a desk for a porter, but he was away from his post. Not sorry to be unobserved, she continued upstairs.

Anthony's flat was easily identified by a card in a small brass holder on the door frame. To her surprise, the door itself was slightly ajar. She knocked lightly.

When no one answered, she pushed the door farther open. Then she gasped, horrified by the sight of bodies lying on the floor of the drawing room that lay just beyond the tiny vestibule. The flat looked like a massacre had taken place.

Then she heard heavy snoring and smelled the sour scent of spilled wine and sickness. Her nostrils flared as she moved forward into the drawing room and examined the scene more carefully. Apparently she had arrived the morning after an orgy. Empty wine bottles were everywhere, along with least a dozen disheveled young men and almost as many women. Not, clearly, the respectable sort of female.

But none of the drunken men were the one she sought. Emma paused uncertainly, knowing that a sensible woman would leave instantly and have strong hysterics outside on the street. But she had already come this far, and she did not want to leave without seeing Anthony. She might not have the courage to return.

An open door at the far end of the drawing room led to a shadowed bedroom. Inside, she could dimly see a bed with a man who might be Anthony sprawled on his back on top of the rumpled counterpane. She preferred not to consider what condition he would be in, or what might be sharing his bed.

She began picking her way among the tangled bodies, doing her best not to touch any. Halfway across the room, one of the sleepers groaned, then rolled over and caught her right ankle. "Nice ankles," he said hazily. "C'mere, darlin'."

He tugged with one hand while his other fumbled with his unbuttoned breeches. She jerked free, stamped smartly on his fingers, and continued toward the bedroom.

A manservant emerged from another door that opened to a small kitchen. He looked appalled at the sight of Emma. "I beg your pardon, miss, b...but his lordship is not receiving."

Emma paused. "Is he in the bedroom?"

"Yes, but this is no place for you!" the valet

exclaimed. "Leave your card, and I'll see that he receives it."

Emma arched her brows and used the manner she had learned from the Dowager Duchess of Warrington. "You needn't be concerned about my reputation. Lord Verlaine is my cousin, so there can be no impropriety in my visit." Ignoring the valet's sputtered protests, she resumed her progress.

Luckily the sleeping man was more or less decent, though his coat and cravat were off and his shirt gaped at the throat, revealing a distracting triangle of bare flesh. Anthony, as handsome as ever, with waving dark hair and the powerful build that looked so much better on Vaughn men than on unfortunate females like her.

She studied the strong-boned, never-forgotten face. It had been so many years. Even in his present condition, rumpled and unshaven, he was magnificent.

Suddenly his eyelids flicked open. She caught her breath, wondering how she could have forgotten the impact of those piercing, light blue eyes. The force of his gaze made her feel like a butterfly pinned in a specimen box.

She was on the verge of flight when he said in a rumbling voice, "You're obviously a Vaughn, but damned if I know which one."

She took a deep breath. "I'm your cousin, Emma Vaughn Stone. You probably don't remember me, but my family always spent Christmas at Harley."

For an endless moment he regarded her unblinkingly.

"Ah, yes. Little Emma Stone. A distant cousin of some sort."

"Second cousin once removed, I believe." She gave him a hesitant smile. "I can't swear to the precise relationship, except to say that it's remote."

He regarded her dourly. "I once fished you out of the lake when you broke through the ice when skating."

"I remember. Not one of my better moments." She had clung to him like a monkey, shivering violently, after he pulled her from the water. He'd immediately carried her up to the house, talking soothingly the whole time. Looking back, that was probably the day she had fallen in love with him.

He sat up and swung his legs over the bed, moving with a caution that said a great deal about his previous night's activities. "Did you come here to play memory lane? If so, your timing is very poor."

She agreed, but now that she had begun, she wanted to get this interview over with quickly. "My purpose is quite different. Would it be possible to have a serious conversation with you?"

He groaned and buried his head in his hands. "Miss Stone, the last thing on earth I want is a serious conversation with anyone."

Perhaps, but he was coherent, and it spoke well for his basic good nature that he could be polite to an unexpected visitor when he probably felt like Vulcan's hammer was pounding on his skull. She turned to the valet, who had been hovering by the door. "Please make a pot of strong coffee for Lord Verlaine."

Years of teaching had given her some skill at persuading the recalcitrant. Very soon she and Anthony were sitting in the tiny kitchen with a pot of coffee on the table between them. Not the best setting for evaluating a potential husband, but at least the kitchen was private.

Anthony had taken the chair by the wall and promptly slumped against the white-washed plaster, three-quarters asleep. She put a steaming mug of coffee in his hand. Eyes closed, he took a deep swallow, his Adam's apple moving. After a second draft, he sighed and opened his eyes. "Miss Stone."

"Emma," she said shyly. "After all, we are cousins. You have known me since I was in the nursery."

"Very well, Emma." He drank more coffee. "To what do I owe the honor of this visit?"

She hesitated, then decided on bluntness. It was her chief talent. "I had heard you were in dire financial straits. On the verge of losing Canfield, in fact."

His expression turning to granite. "Our relationship is nowhere near close enough for you to speak of such matters. I'll thank you to leave now."

She swallowed hard. Angry, he was formidable. "I'm sorry. I know that was impertinent. I only ask because... perhaps I can help."

"No one can help," he snapped. "In three days, the mortgages will come due and the property will be taken from me. For two years, ever since my father died, I've been trying to pay off his damned debts, and now it's too late."

Her eyes widened. Anthony's father had been a charming, amiable fellow, but she remembered whispers that he was a gamester. "So your gambling has been an attempt to earn enough to pay off the mortgages."

Anthony's eyes narrowed. "How the devil did you know that? Even my best friends have assumed that I was playing only for sport."

She shrugged, unable to explain. "An educated guess."

He poured more coffee and added milk, his expression haggard. Desolate, even. "I needed forty thousand pounds. I'd managed to accumulate half that. There was no chance of borrowing more—believe me, I'd tried. My father's history of gambling made the banks consider me a poor risk. With only a few days until foreclosure, I had to throw caution to the winds." His eyes closed with pain. "Yesterday I bet the whole amount on a single game, double or nothing. If I'd won, Canfield would have been saved."

There was a hushed silence before she spoke the obvious. "But you didn't win."

His mouth twisted. "The cards were against me. The Deity, if there is one, apparently didn't want to see me remain a landowner."

"So you are not a gamester by temperament," she said thoughtfully.

"Believe me, if Canfield was secure, I'd never pick up another deck of cards in my life!" he said bitterly. "My father did enough gambling for both of us."

She did believe him. Her hands locked around her mug until the knuckles whitened. The worst charge against Anthony was that he was a hopeless gambler, but if that wasn't true, it changed everything. "Perhaps... perhaps we could help each other. I have just come into an unexpected legacy. I would like to marry and have a family, but as a governess I've had no opportunity to meet eligible men."

She stopped to gather her courage before continuing, "Purely by chance, my solicitor mentioned that your property was on the verge of foreclosure. Since I am in need of a husband and you are in need of a fortune, I...I thought perhaps you might be willing to consider a...a marriage of convenience."

"What?" His mug, which was halfway to his mouth, slammed down on the table and scalding coffee slopped across his hand. "You want me to *marry* you?"

His appalled expression was worse than a slap in the face. How could she have been so brazen, so *stupid,* as to suggest that a handsome, fashionable man like him might consider marrying a woman like her?

Face burning, she jumped up and grabbed her cloak from the back of her chair. "It was just a thought, and obviously a bad one. I'm sorry for disturbing you, Anthony. Lord Verlaine." She turned and bolted toward the kitchen door.

His chair scraped the floor, and in one bound he crossed the kitchen and caught her arm. "Wait! I'm sorry, Emma. I intended no insult." He turned her to face him. "This is just so...so unexpected."

Though she was a tall woman, he loomed over her, intimidatingly large. The reality of him was very different from her hazy childhood memories. He was a man now, not a youth. A man who was strong, virile, and forceful. For a woman who'd lived the last decade in a world of women and children, the effect was rather overpowering.

Her gaze went to his unshaved chin. The dark stubble was surprisingly intriguing. She wanted to touch it, discover the texture of those very masculine whiskers.

She wrenched her gaze away. "I'm sorry. It was presumptuous of me to march in like this."

"Unusual, perhaps, but not presumptuous." He studied her, his gaze piercing. "I keep wondering if I'm dreaming this whole scene out of a desperate desire to save Canfield."

"This is no dream," she said with conviction. He was too vivid, his hand on her arm too warm and strong, for this encounter to be anything but real.

He released her arm and made a courtly gesture toward the table. "Come sit down again, Cousin. You were quite right to say we must have a serious conversation."

CHAPTER 3

ANTHONY VAUGHN POURED MORE coffee for himself and his guest. Even after two cups, he still felt he was standing next door to death. He shouldn't have drunk himself into a stupor last night, and he definitely shouldn't have invited so many of his rackety friends to join in a perverse celebration of his disastrous gaming loss. He wondered vaguely when the whores had come. There had been none present when he passed out.

He put that aside to concentrate on more important matters, namely, his amazing cousin, who sat across from him looking every inch the meek, dowdy governess. Yet it must have taken courage for her to come here and make her startling proposition.

Thinking back, he remembered her as a quiet child who tagged around after him with huge, speaking eyes. But there had been many children at Harley during the holidays. Except for the incident on the ice, he recalled very little about Emma.

First things first. He said, "You have forty thousand pounds?"

After a moment's hesitation, she said, "If we were to marry, you would immediately have fifty thousand pounds at your disposal."

It was enough to save Canfield, and make necessary improvements as well. Enough to live like a gentleman again. But still—marriage? It was a state he had not contemplated since dear damned Cecilia .

He studied his long-lost cousin intently. When he'd first seen her picking her way through the tangled bodies of his dissolute friends with cat-like care, he'd thought he was hallucinating. But he could not have imagined such a startling mixture of shyness and candor. She had the Vaughn height, square jaw, and dark hair. Though no beauty, she was presentable, or would be when decently dressed.

That was all very well for a cousin, but a wife? Yet what were his choices? Marry this disconcertingly direct but not unpleasant woman, or lose Canfield.

Put in those terms, there was really no choice at all. As a boy, he'd taken for granted that Canfield would be his one day. It wasn't until his father's death, when he realized that he was on the verge of losing the estate, that he had recognized how much he loved the place. More than loved—in a very real way, being Verlaine of Canfield defined him. Without it, he was merely an idle, careless fellow of good birth and small accomplishment, as useless as a dandelion.

He said carefully, "If you want children, it would have to be more than a marriage of convenience."

Emma turned beet red and looked away. "I understand that, of course. What I meant was that it would not be a love match."

An understatement. He asked, "What would you expect of me in the way of husbandly duties?" When she blushed again, he added, "I mean that in the broadest possible sense."

She thought before replying. "If we were to marry, I would ask that you treat me with courtesy and consideration, especially in front of others. I do not want to become a laughingstock—the desperate woman who bought herself a husband who cannot care for her." Her voice was rich and smooth as fine brandy, surprisingly provocative for a woman of her very proper appearance.

"That is hardly a problem. I would be no kind of gentleman if I treated you any other way," he remarked. "What else?"

Her gaze dropped. "Though I want children very much, I would prefer for that part of the marriage to be delayed until we are...are better acquainted."

A little relieved, he said, "A quite understandable desire. Do you have any other requirements?"

She shook her head mutely.

"If that is all you want, you would be a very easily pleased wife," he said dryly. "If we do agree to this, we would need to marry immediately, within the next two day, for me to save Canfield. Would you mind that?"

After a brief hesitation, she said, "Not under these circumstances."

He sighed and bent his head, running his fingers through his tangled hair. Marriage was for life. It was not a commitment he had ever thought to make to a virtual stranger. That was why he hadn't looked around for an heiress when he discovered his financial problems. And, of course, he'd thought he would be able to save Canfield through his own efforts.

But how much did one person ever really know another? He'd thought he'd known Cecilia , and been pitifully wrong. Emma Stone would probably make an easy, sensible wife, and she was not quite a stranger. Growing up in the same extended family surely counted for something.

He raised his gaze and studied his cousin again. Her face was so pale that a ghostly scattering of freckles showed across her high cheekbones. She was as nervous as he, and with good reason. When a woman married, she gave her body, her name, and her worldly goods to her husband. Perhaps that was why Emma had made her proposal to a man with whom she had at least some acquaintance.

Honor compelled him to say, "Are you absolutely sure you want this, Emma? My situation is urgent, but yours is not. You're young. You can afford to take more time searching for the mate who will best please you." His mouth curved without humor. "Remember the old saying, 'Marry in haste, repent at leisure.'"

Her gaze slid away from his. "I could spend years

looking, but it wouldn't guarantee a better decision in the end. A man eager to marry a fortune is bound to make himself agreeable during the courtship. How would I know his true nature? With you, at least, I know that you are pleasant to servants and patient with small brats who follow you around."

Bemused, he said, "Did I call you a brat?"

"Yes, though not unkindly." She smiled a little. "Younger children are more aware of older ones than vice versa. It's not surprising that you scarcely remember me, while I recall you quite vividly."

Though Emma had courage and honesty, her opinion of her own worth was not high, he realized. His shock when she'd suggested marriage had hurt her badly. Obviously she didn't think a man would marry her for any reason except money.

His thoughtful gaze went over her full, womanly figure. While his preference was for ethereal blondes, it would be no hardship to lie with Emma. No hardship at all. If he satisfied her in bed and treated her with courtesy everywhere else, she would be content with this marriage. As for him—he would have Canfield.

He hesitated a moment longer, knowing that his life was about to change forever in ways that he couldn't even imagine. Then he took Emma's cold hand between both of his and said very formally, "My dearest cousin, would you do me the honor of becoming my wife?"

Face pale, she said, "The honor will be mine, Anthony."

The deal was done.

Heavy silence fell between them. Having agreed to marry, what came next? Anthony said, "I must call on your solicitor and discuss the financial settlements. I'll also go to Doctors' Commons for a special license, and arrange for the ceremony to take place day after tomorrow. Do you have any preference as to place or time?"

She shook her head. "Whatever is convenient. I'm staying at Grillon's Hotel. You may notify me of your arrangements there." She pulled paper and pencil from her reticule and printed out a name and address. "My solicitor."

After handing him the paper, she got to her feet. "I'll leave you now. You have much to do."

She was right, and he was going to have to do it while suffering from the prince of hangovers. He stood, thinking there should be something more to commemorate such a significant occasion. He took her hand again. "Until our wedding day, Emma."

She flinched when he dropped a light kiss on her hand. He hoped that she wasn't one of those women with a constitutional dislike of physical intimacy. Well, it was too late to worry about that now. He would have to hope that his proven expertise with the fair sex would not fail him.

Taking her arm, he escorted her to his front door. Several of his friends were beginning to wake up, usually accompanied by low moans. His valet, Hawkins, had wisely set basins near the afflicted. Emma did a fine job of ignoring the whole decadent scene. Really a most sensible woman.

He squeezed her hand meaningfully at the front door, and she left him with a shy smile. Halfway back to his bedroom, one of his rackety friends, Matthews, muttered, "That must be the ugliest whore in London. Very proper of you to throw her out."

A surge of unexpected anger burned through Anthony. He bent over and grabbed Matthews's shirt front in both hands, lifting him half off the floor. "You are speaking of my affianced wife," he said in his most menacing tone. "Do I make myself clear?"

Matthews's eyes widened until they resembled bloodshot gooseberries. "S...sorry, Verlaine! No insult intended, upon my word, no indeed!"

He was still babbling apologies when Anthony dropped him back to the floor and returned to his bedroom. Mercifully, Hawkins had left a pitcher of hot water on the washstand. As Anthony splashed water on his face, his spirits began to rise. Canfield was saved. The Lord moved in mysterious ways His wonders to perform, and the Deity had outdone himself today.

TWO DAYS LATER, Emma donned her Sunday best dress for her wedding. Becky suggested a more elaborate hairstyle, but Emma rejected it on the grounds that she would look silly. She did spare a wistful thought for her childhood dreams of a romantic courtship, an adoring bridegroom, and a ceremony in the Harley chapel where she would be surrounded by fond relatives. But those things were trivial. What mattered was that she was marrying Anthony, a fact so wonderful that she had never dreamed about it, at least not seriously.

At eleven o'clock punctually, Mr. Evans came for Emma and Becky. He had agreed to be a witness to the ceremony, while Becky would be maid of honor. On the short ride to the local parish church, Emma asked, "What did you think of Anthony?"

The solicitor said cautiously, "While I cannot approve of such haste, I was not unfavorably impressed by the young gentleman. He has a good head on him, and he was very reasonable about the settlements. Very reasonable indeed."

High praise from a lawyer. The carriage halted in front of the church, and she descended into drizzly rain. It would have been nice if the sun had come out, she thought wistfully. Everything about this wedding was drab and hurried.

Telling herself again that the details didn't matter, she entered the church, and saw that Anthony had already arrived with a friend to be groomsman. Elegantly dressed in a dark blue coat and immaculately starched cravat, he was so handsome that she almost bolted from the church. How could a barnyard hen mate with a lordly peacock?

Then Anthony saw her and came down the aisle with a smile. He was carrying a small nosegay in one hand. Presenting it to her, he said, "I thought you might like these."

The flowers were tiny winter roses, white mixed with

palest pink and bound together with a silver ribbon. Heaven only knew where he'd found them in December. The exquisite blossoms made the rest of the ceremony's shortcomings fade into irrelevance. "Oh, Anthony," she breathed. "They're perfect."

All doubts gone, she took his arm and they walked together to the vicar. This marriage was right. She knew it.

CHAPTER 4

THE NEWLYWEDS HAD their first quarrel shortly after the wedding breakfast. Mr. Evans and Anthony's groomsman left after they'd all shared an excellent meal in a private room at Grillon's Hotel. Since Anthony's bachelor rooms were hardly suitable for a new wife, he had engaged a suite at the hotel. One with two bedrooms. As he'd thought dryly when booking the rooms, the least he could do with Emma's money was use it to ensure that she was comfortable. His valet and her maid had moved the necessary personal belongings into the suite, then been given the rest of the day off.

As Anthony escorted Emma up to the suite, he considered carrying her across the threshold. He decided against it since this would not be their home, and the gesture seemed entirely too intimate at their present stage of acquaintance. Ironic to feel that way about his wife on their wedding night.

He had another fleeting thought, this time about Cecilia . The only time he'd ever thought about wedding nights had been when he'd thought they would marry. She had been beautiful—small and graceful and blonde, the complete antithesis of Emma. He immediately suppressed the thought as disloyal.

As they stepped into their handsome sitting room, he said lightly, "Welcome to our temporary home, Emma Vaughn Stone Vaughn." He smiled. "Lady Verlaine."

Smiling, she removed her bonnet. "That's rather too many Vaughns, isn't it?"

"Exactly the right number." He pulled a set of papers from inside his coat. "Here, Emma, a wedding present of sorts. The paid-off mortgages on Canfield."

After a brief glance, she handed the documents back. "I'm glad."

He set the papers aside. "With the mortgages cleared, the property will soon be producing a very comfortable income. I'm letting go the rooms on Bruton Street, but within a year or two, we should be able to afford a house here in town if you'd like that."

"That would be nice, but for now I'm looking forward to living at Canfield."

He nodded. "It will be good to be back. I thought we could go early next week."

Her dark brows drew together. "Wouldn't it be easier to go direct from London to Harley Castle? Canfield is almost the opposite direction."

Startled, he said, "Harley? We aren't going there."

"We aren't?" She stared at him in dismay. "Whyever

not? It's been ten years since I've been able to attend one of the Christmas gatherings. I...I've been looking forward to returning."

His face tightened. "I haven't been for nine years myself, and I have no intention of going now."

She slowly sank onto the sofa. "All this time I've imagined you at the castle with the rest of the family every Christmas. Why did you stop attending?"

"I doubted that I'd be welcome," he said brusquely.

She gazed at him with her large, changeable eyes, which were a smoky gray at the moment. "How could that be?"

Could she really not know? Remembering that her parents had died suddenly and she had disappeared from the family circle, he supposed it was possible. "You never heard that Cousin Cecilia married Brand?"

"Brand!" Emma exclaimed. "But I always thought that you and she would make a match of it. I...I did wonder what had happened when I learned you were unwed, but I had no idea that she'd married Lord Brandon instead."

Edward Alexander Vaughn, Marquess of Brandon, their mutual cousin. Heir to the Duke of Warrington, and once, long ago, Anthony's closest friend. "Why shouldn't she marry Brand?" he said with acid humor. "He will have far more wealth and a much better title, and he always doted on her."

Emma gazed at him, her eyes darkening. "I see."

She probably *did* see; the damned woman seemed able to read his mind. It gave her an unfair advantage.

Her gaze dropped and she slowly peeled off her

gloves. "I shall write the Dowager Duchess again and say that we cannot come after all."

The dowager duchess was Brand's grandmother, and the benevolent silver-haired despot of Harley and the whole sprawling Vaughn family. Anthony felt a pang as he thought of her elegant presence and dry humor. Since she no longer came to London, he hadn't seen her in nine years. He missed her. "You'd already written an acceptance?"

"Yesterday. I told her of our planned marriage and said we would arrive next week." Emma sighed. "I'm sorry. It never occurred to me that we would not be going."

Despite her calm words, Emma's disappointment was palpable. He prowled around the drawing room, feeling like a complete villain. Though he no longer went to Harley, he hadn't suffered during the intervening years. He'd finished his education at Oxford, gone on a Grand Tour after Waterloo made the Continent safe for Englishmen again, and generally enjoyed the life of a privileged young gentleman right up until financial disaster had struck.

During those same years, Emma had been living a miserable existence as a teacher and governess, probably sleeping in icy garret rooms and stoically enduring employers who weren't worthy to tie her shoes. It was all too easy to imagine her secretly dreaming of happier days at Harley. And they *had* been happy days—the best of Anthony's life. He felt another pang. God, why had everything gone so wrong?

Even as the question formed in his mind, he reminded himself that the fault for that was his. Nor die he have the right to deny his wife what she so much desired merely because he'd acted like an idiot many years earlier.

For a cowardly moment he considered telling Emma to go alone, but that would be contemptible and unfair to her. He stopped pacing and turned to her. "If you are set on the visit, I suppose we must go. I am too much in your debt to refuse."

Instead of looking grateful, she said, "Don't say that. Indebtedness is a poor foundation for a marriage. You will soon hate feeling obligated, and then you will hate me." Her lips curved in a wry smile. "I don't want that."

He felt as if he'd just been struck a solid blow to the midriff. Who would have thought that this woman, whom a week earlier he would have passed on the street without a second glance, would be able to get into his mind so effortlessly? After drawing a deep breath, he said, "You are very wise, and very generous."

"Not really. The bargain we struck is a fair one. My money paid the debts incurred by your father, and in return I have secured a fine home and a distinguished rank in society." A hint of irony sounded in her husky voice. "Not to mention a husband that all women will envy me."

"I shall do my best to forget my sense of obligation," he said, thinking she over-rated his desirability. When he was trying to raise money to save Canfield, parents had kept their eligible daughters far away. "I'll be a properly arrogant husband in no time."

Her face lit up as she laughed. He realized that he hadn't seen her laugh before. Amusement transformed her from sober governess to a vividly alive woman.

That realization was followed by another: he *wanted* to take her to Harley. Not because he was in her debt, but because he wanted to please her, since she asked so little for herself. "Since you've already written to the Dowager Duchess, we really ought to go to Harley. I promise I won't be a martyr over it."

She caught her breath, hope in her eyes. "Are you sure? I really don't want to go if a visit would be painful for you."

Ruefully he recognized that his accommodating wife was making it easy for him to be a coward. He must take care that she didn't undermine what character he possessed. "I expect that the visit will be awkward, at least at the beginning. But actually, having just married makes this the perfect time to return. If I don't now, I may be condemning myself to a lifetime of exile. I've just realized that I don't want that. Harley and the family gatherings were too important a part of my life to throw away without at least attempting to mend those burned bridges." His tone turned dry. "Of course, Brand may throw me out, but at least I will have tried."

Surprised, Emma said, "Surely he would not behave so rudely. I remember him as being very even-tempered."

Anthony hesitated, reluctant to lose his bride's good opinion, but knowing it would be unfair to take her to

Harley without telling her the whole story. "Even a steady man reacts badly to being told his adored fiancée is marrying him for his money and title. That every night he and Cecilia lay together, she'd be thinking of me."

Emma winced. "Anthony, you didn't."

He sighed. "I'm afraid I did, along with some other equally insulting comments. We got into a ferocious fight. I'm bigger, but Brand was murderously angry. If our fathers hadn't intervened, it might have ended in pistols at dawn."

"Thank heaven it didn't come to that!" she said vehemently.

"I wouldn't want Brand's blood on my head," he agreed.

Amused, she said, "You're that sure you would have won?"

"I'm a far better shot." He had a brief, horrifying image of him and Brand facing each other with pistols in their hands. Thank God that hadn't happened.

"But if there had been a duel, wouldn't the choice of weapons have been Brand's? As I recall, he was a superb swordsman."

She was right, he realized. "I never thought of that, probably because the quarrel didn't go so far. I left Harley the same day, and have never been back. Once or twice Brand and I have met in public. He always gives me the cut direct."

"So much has happened that I never knew about," she said pensively.

He resumed his prowling as he thought about the

return to Harley. Brand's parents and grandmother would not allow any scenes, but the situation would still be strained. Sadly he thought of all the boyhood escapades he and his cousin had shared. They'd gone to school together at Winchester. Countless nights had been spent commiserating about the horrors of school, or sneaking out to buy the extra food necessary to growing boys.

That closeness was no longer possible, not with the shadows of Cecilia and Anthony's own insulting behavior between them. But if he apologized profusely, perhaps they could at least be civil to each other in the future.

Lord, what would it be like to see Cecilia again? He wasn't sure if he loved her or despised her. Both, perhaps. She was the only girl he'd ever loved, and she'd made a fool of him. Her betrayal had left permanent scars. If financial necessity hadn't driven him to marry Emma, it was quite possible that he would have spent his life as a bachelor.

He ceased his prowling and studied his wife, who still sat peaceably on the sofa, giving no hint of her thoughts. He felt a curious duality. He liked her, and his respect for her intelligence and honesty was growing hourly.

At the same time, he saw her as the drab governess whose appearance had been designed to avoid notice. She had been right to say that people would wonder why the fashionable Lord Verlaine had married such an unprepossessing woman.

After a moment spent deciding how to present his case in a way so that would not sound too insulting, he said, "You asked to be treated with courtesy and respect for the sake of your pride. I, too, have pride. I don't want to go to Harley and have the family judge me a fortune hunter who has taken advantage of your honesty and innocence."

Her expression closed. "Does that you mean you've again changed your mind about going there?"

"It means that we'll both benefit by appearing fond rather than barely acquainted. And that we must get you to a modiste and order you a new wardrobe immediately."

Taken aback, she said, "I wouldn't object to some new gowns. But you can't make a silk purse from a sow's ear."

Uncomfortably aware that she had sensed what he wasn't saying, he said, "How fortunate that we don't have to. Come. I'll take you to Madame Chloe. There's no time to waste if we're to have you turned out properly by next week."

"Very well." She got to her feet and retrieved her bonnet, saying darkly, "Just remember what I said about sow's ears!"

"Actually, your ears are quite well-shaped and attractive," he said thoughtfully. "After your gowns are ordered, we must stop at the jewelers for some earrings that will do them justice."

As she blushed and pulled on her gloves, he realized that he was looking forward to playing Pygmalion to her Galatea.

❄

EMMA'S MOTHER had spoken enthusiastically of the joys of visiting a London modiste, but that was one of many experiences that poverty had stolen from Emma. She tried not to gawk when Anthony swept her into Madame Chloe's shop. The luxuriously decorated salon reminded her of the dowager duchess's boudoir. In such a temple of feminine fashion and frivolity, Anthony's powerful, broad-shouldered figure looked almost indecently masculine.

Madame Chloe herself, a handsome woman of mature years, came forward to greet them, her expression brightening at the sight of Anthony. With a trace of French accent, she said, "Milord Verlaine. What a pleasure to see you again."

As Emma tried not to think what other women her husband had brought to the salon, he said breezily, "The pleasure is mutual, Madame. Our visit is something of an emergency. My wife's trunks were destroyed in a fire at a coaching inn." He shook his head sadly. "She was forced to borrow clothing from the vicar's wife, a worthy woman, but not fashionable. Everything must be replaced, from the skin out."

Chloe may or may not have believed his lie, but she laughed good-naturedly. "You have come to the right place." Her eyes narrowed critically as she studied Emma. "You have a really lovely complexion, Lady Verlaine. And your figure! *Magnifique.*"

Emma blinked. It was true that her skin was nice, but her figure was altogether too....too much. Definitely not the figure of a fashionable sylph. Meekly she said, "I put myself in your hands, madam."

Without further ado, she was whisked off to a private alcove. Luckily, Anthony did not accompany them. Chloe gave whispered instructions to an assistant, who darted off. By the time Emma had been stripped down to her shift and measured, the assistant had returned from a nearby shop with a mound of exquisitely sewn under things.

Emma donned a lovely new lawn shift, then allowed herself to be laced into a set of surprisingly comfortable quilted dimity stays. Chloe explained sorrowfully that it would take several days to make proper shifts and other garments, and that she hoped milady was not too offended at having to make do with ready-made items. Emma was hard pressed not to laugh. The unmentionables that the modiste was apologizing for were the finest she'd worn in many years.

Madame Chloe held up a shimmering green garment. "This gown is being made for another client who is of similar size and figure. She will not mind if you try it on for just a moment to get the effect."

Emma raised her arms, and whispering green silk dropped over her. After the fastenings were secured, she turned to look at herself in the mirror. Her jaw dropped. The image she saw was not of the familiar dowdy governess, but a striking, fashionable woman. Even her eyes were unfamiliar as the green gown made them glow like jade. Voice hushed, she asked, "Is this really me?"

"Indeed, my lady. It is the real you," Chloe said with satisfaction. "Lord Verlaine will be most pleased."

Then the modiste swept Emma into the main salon so her husband could survey the results. Emma was tempted to cover the large expanse of bare flesh visible above her décolletage, but managed to restrain herself. The problem was not with the gown, but her unfashionable self.

Anthony was gazing out the window at the afternoon traffic outside, his expression pensive. When she entered the main salon, he turned and became very still. After a long moment, he said softly, "Well, well, *well*."

"It's the stays," Emma blurted out. "I'm not really shaped like this."

He grinned as he circled around her. "My dear, no woman is shaped precisely like that, which is why stays were invented. And believe me, you shape up very well."

She blushed to the roots of her hair. But she was not displeased. She studied herself in the salon mirrors. She was not a delicate fashionable beauty, and she never would be. But she had a kind of forceful splendor that made her a woman who would not be easily overlooked. It was a heady thought.

Emma clung to that satisfaction through a long, tiring afternoon while endless fabrics and patterns were chosen. By the time they left, she was exhausted. In the carriage, she sank into the velvet squabs of the seat. "What a very unusual wedding day."

Anthony chuckled. "It was time well spent.

Tomorrow we'll visit jewelers and find you shoes and stockings and such like. The other important thing is your hair."

He leaned forward and removed her bonnet, then pulled out the pins that secured the knot on her nape. Her hair tumbled over her shoulders. Gently he brushed the dark waves back, the skim of his fingertips on her ear and throat sending sparks through her. She caught her breath, shocked that such a casual touch could stir her so.

Apparently unaffected, he said, "Tomorrow, a hairdresser. Your maid—Becky, I think?—must come with us to learn how to do new styles."

It all sounded wonderful, but Emma could not dismiss a flash of concern. "Anthony, can we afford all this?"

He frowned, and for a moment she feared that her question had angered him. But his voice was even when he said, "Your wardrobe will cost a pretty penny, but it's a necessary expenditure, one that I allowed for when estimating our expenses. You must trust me when I say that I have no desire to live in debt again, Emma."

She gazed at him, enchanted by his serious expression, the way his attention was concentrated on her. This glorious male creature was now her husband. *Hers.* "I trust you, Anthony," she said softly. "Never doubt it."

She had never been happier in her life.

THE DOWAGER DUCHESS of Warrington chose her moment carefully. The Vaughns were just finishing dinner, but it was not yet time to rise. Her gaze went over her beloved family. Her son James, the duke, with his quiet dignity and dry humor. Her daughter-in-law Amelia, a woman of wit and laughing charm. Sarah, her youngest granddaughter, who would be presented to society in the spring.

The dowager's eyes clouded when she looked at her grandson, Alexander, who would be the next duke, and his wife, Cecilia. Oh, they'd produced two fine boys dutifully enough, but something was wrong between them, and both were too pigheaded to ask advice from those who were older and wiser.

Concealing her thoughts, the dowager said, "I've received most of the replies for the Christmas gathering. Besides the usual guests, there will be a few who are less expected."

She took a sip of wine as every gaze turned to her. Setting down the crystal goblet, she said, "Verlaine will be coming with his new wife."

Her statement produced absolute silence. The duke and his wife exchanged a swift, startled glance. Brand's face became as expressionless as marble while Cecilia 's gaze dropped to the meringue swan on her plate. Only Lady Sarah, too young to remember what had happened, said brightly, "Cousin Anthony? Marvelous! He hasn't come for Christmas in donkeys' years. Who did he marry?"

"A Vaughn connection, actually," the dowager replied. "Emma Stone. The daughter of your second cousin, James. She used to come with her parents, Jane Vaughn and Sir George Stone. They both died of a fever ten years back. Luckily the girl was at school, or she might have died, too. She has not been here since then."

Amelia pursed her lips. "Jane Stone's daughter. I remember her. A nice child. Quiet, but with very speaking eyes and excellent manners."

James said with a barely discernible hint of irony, "How pleasant it will be to see them both again." He studied his son, who had said nothing. "I didn't realize that you still sent invitations to such distant relatives, *Maman*."

"That is why family gatherings should be left in the hands of the old," she said serenely. "We have the time and memory to maintain the family connections. It wasn't easy keeping track of Emma, but I made sure that she received an invitation every year. She would always return a pretty note, regretting that she could not attend."

"I shall be glad to see Emma," Cecilia said with a touch of defiance. "I've wondered what had become of her. She was nice, and so clever. How lovely that she and Anthony have discovered each other after so many years." She cast a wistful glance at her husband, but he would not look at her. A muscle jerked in his jaw as he stared at the tapestry on the opposite wall.

Slowly the dowager drank the last of her wine.

Though fireworks were not traditional at Christmas, they would certainly take place at Harley this year. God willing, they'd shed some light in corners too long filled with shadow.

EMMA EYED a piece of toast doubtfully. "I don't think I can eat. I'm too excited at the thought that today we're actually going to Harley."

Her husband picked up the toast and put it in her hand. "Eat," he ordered. "You'll make yourself ill if you set off on a long coach trip with an empty stomach."

Pleased by his concern, she obediently spread honey on the toast and took a bite. It did taste good. Her gaze went around the attractive room. In the week of their hotel honeymoon, she'd grown fond of the place. Every morning their breakfast was served on a small table in a corner of the drawing room. Several newspapers arrived at the same time, and she and Anthony had fallen into the habit of sharing a leisurely meal, reading and discussing the news of the day.

Her husband had been surprised the first time she'd offered an opinion, but he'd adjusted very quickly. Now he seemed to enjoy their discussions as much as she did.

Later in the day, after they had done the shopping and fittings necessary to her transformation, he would take her to see sights that she'd had no chance to visit when she was working.

Her gaze went to the doors that led to the two bedrooms. In that area, their honeymoon was sadly deficient. Anthony was always charming and considerate, but he'd made no attempts to bed his bride. Was he taking her desire to wait too seriously, or was he simply not very interested?

Granted, before their hasty wedding Emma had felt skittish about giving herself to a near-stranger, but time was rapidly curing her of that. The yearning she'd felt for Anthony when she was a girl had returned ten-fold. She loved every casual touch, even if he was only helping her from the carriage. She loved looking at him, studying the strong planes of his face, his easy, athletic movements. She delighted in small discoveries like the faint scar on his chin, and enjoyed the irrepressible tuft of hair that lived its own life, wild and free, no matter what Anthony did to try and tame it.

Her husband divided the last of the coffee—another taste they shared—between their cups. "Do you know, my worst fear when we married was that we wouldn't have anything to say to each other," he said thoughtfully. "But I've noticed no shortage of conversation."

She gave him a smile of suspicious innocence. "That's because you're so extremely interesting that there is always something to discuss."

"Flatterer," he laughed, his gaze warm. "You have a wicked sense of humor."

For a moment, she wondered if he was going to lean forward and kiss her. Apart from the briefest of pecks at their wedding ceremony, they hadn't kissed at all.

After a suspended moment, he drained his coffee and got to his feet. "I'll go order the carriage and summon porters for the baggage. We must be off soon if we wish to make Harley in one day."

She nodded, suppressing her disappointment. Having asked for time to ease into the intimacy of marriage, she supposed she had no right to complain at receiving more than she'd bargained for.

THEY MADE GOOD TIME, and arrived at Harley just as full dark was settling over the rolling hills. As they rattled up the long driveway, Emma peered out the carriage window. "Look! The Christmas candles are lit. I'd forgotten about them."

Anthony looked past her and saw a lattice of lights, one candle in every window of the massive building. There was enough moonlight to recognize the pale stone and graceful proportions of one of Britain's grandest homes. It was a palace, really, almost as large as Blenheim or Castle Howard. "I'd half forgotten the candles, too. Yet now that I see them, they remind me of everything I've ever loved about Harley."

"I'd given up believing that I'd ever return," Emma

said softly. "Now that I'm here, I'm frightened. I've lived in a different world for the last ten years. I don't belong at Harley anymore. I keep thinking that the dowager only invited me from courtesy, believing I would never accept."

The darkness made it easy for him to reach out and take her gloved hand. It was large and capable and well-formed, like the rest of Emma. "Even if that were true, which it isn't, you would still be welcome here as my wife." He stopped suddenly, struck by the irony of his words. "That was a foolish statement, wasn't it? I'm the one wondering if I'll be thrown out bodily."

Her hand tightened on his. "Of course not. It's been nine years. You say that Brand and Cecilia have two children now. He probably barely remembers your fight."

Anthony wished he believed that. But he didn't.

Their carriage pulled up in front of wide, torch-lit steps. Instantly footmen emerged to take their baggage. With a steady stream of Vaughns arriving, the servants had their routine down to a fine art. While two footmen went for the baggage, another opened the carriage door and flipped down the folding step. Anthony climbed out first, then turned to assist Emma. She gave him a tremulous smile as she stepped down.

She looked so vulnerable that he wanted to take her in his arms and murmur comforting words in one elegant ear. In fact, he would like to take her in his arms anyhow. She had blossomed under the ministrations of Madame Chloe, the best hairdresser in London, and sundry jewelers, shoemakers, and others.

Under his breath, he whispered, "You look every inch a Vaughn."

Her smile widened and became more confident. Arm in arm, they climbed the steps. A footman opened the massive front door and bowed them in. No sooner had they entered the huge, three-story entry hall when a gaggle of children, aged between about six and twelve, ran shrieking through the far end of the space. By the time Anthony blinked, they'd come and gone.

Emma laughed as her gaze went to the fragrant greenery and bright ribbons that decorated the hall. "Lord, that brings back memories. Remember how exciting it was to arrive here see all the cousins for the first time in a year?"

"Vividly." On his last visit, the cousin Anthony had longed for most had been Cecilia. Tonight he would see her again. The thought knotted his stomach.

Before Anthony could say more, a comfortable looking woman of middle years came forward to greet them. It was the Duchess of Warrington herself, Brand's mother. "Anthony, how wonderful to see you again," she said warmly. "And Emma, how splendid you look. It's hard to believe you're so grown up."

She kissed Emma's cheek, then turned and offered her hand to Anthony. As he bowed over it, she said with a twinkle, "The dowager and Cecilia and I have been taking turns receiving people since yesterday morning. I'm so glad that you two arrived on my shift. Having you both here again is quite the most exciting event this Christmas."

Emma said quietly, "I can't tell you how much it means to be at Harley again."

Anthony added, "How is everyone? The duke, the dowager" After the faintest of pauses, he added, "Brand. Cecilia. Your daughters."

The duchess's mouth twisted ruefully. "Brand is... stubborn. Cecilia and her boys are very well. Anne and her husband arrived earlier today, and you won't even recognize my Sarah. She's all grown and chafing to be presented."

Three chattering females entered the hall. The oldest called out exuberantly, "Verlaine, you rascal, what's this about a wife?"

"Aunt Fanny!" Anthony exclaimed, giving her a big hug. Turning to the younger women, he said, "And these dazzling creatures must be my cousins Rebecca and Louisa."

Both girls giggled, and Louisa hugged Anthony. When he emerged from her embrace, he said, "You already know my wife. She was Emma Stone, you know."

His Aunt Fanny, actually a first cousin once removed, said in a booming voice, "Of course I remember little Emma. Not that you're so little now." Her gaze went over the subject of the discussion. "Pure Vaughn," she pronounced. "Has Verlaine got you with child yet, girl?"

As Emma turned scarlet, Anthony recalled that Fanny had always been an earthy sort. Putting one arm around his wife's shoulders, he said firmly, "Behave yourself, Aunt Fanny. We haven't been married even a fortnight yet."

Fanny shook her head with regret. "You should have

waited and had the wedding here. Always good to have another reason to celebrate."

The duchess intervened, saying, "We've never lacked for celebration, Fanny. Now let me take these young people to their room so they can freshen up." She whisked Anthony and Emma up the sweeping stairs.

As they climbed, she said with a mischievous smile, "You're the last to arrive. The house is packed to the rafters. As newlyweds, I'm sure you won't mind sharing a bedroom."

Anthony darted a look at Emma. She looked startled, and rather alarmed. That was something they'd both overlooked—with the house full, married couples were required to share quarters. Since many of them were used to having separate rooms, there were always good-natured complaints about the crowding.

They had to climb three flights of steps to reach their room. There were no less than four stops to greet other Vaughns who were coming and going along the halls and stairs. Anthony was better remembered, not only because he'd already reached adulthood on his last visits, but because he'd always been outgoing. But Emma was greeted warmly, too. The exuberant welcomes created the holiday spirit she remembered so well. Though not every member of the family loved every other member, for the next fortnight, there was goodwill enough for all.

When they reached their assigned chamber the duchess said, "Because so many guests have just arrived today, dinner will not be formal." She smiled. "Not much changes here, you know. Tomorrow will be a formal dinner, the night after is Christmas Eve and the service in the chapel. And so it will go until the Twelfth Night ball."

"The events might not change, but the people do," Emma observed. "This will be my first time dining with the adults rather than at the children's table."

"Why, so it is. You were still in the schoolroom the last time you came for Christmas." The duchess's expression became grave. "Such a terrible thing, your parents' deaths. *Maman* and I were sorry that you would not come to us afterward. But you obviously decided wisely, for you are blooming now." She turned to leave. "I mustn't keep you talking. It isn't much more than half an hour until we dine. You remember the bell, I'm sure."

"Who could forget it?" Anthony said feelingly. He took the duchess's hands. "Thank you for having us here, Aunt Amelia."

"The pleasure is mine. Family is the touchstone of life. We're fortunate that Harley is large enough to hold so many Vaughns. I think of us as traveling through time together. There are constant changes—births, marriages, deaths—yet as a family, we are whole and healthy." With a last smile, the duchess left.

When they were alone, Emma removed her bonnet, saying, "As a child I wished that the towers were round, not square, but this is still one of the nicest rooms in Harley."

"We must have received it because of our status as newlyweds," Anthony replied. With typical Harley efficiency, their baggage had already been delivered. While he and Emma had socialized, her maid and his man had done the unpacking and vanished again. The mechanics of life always flowed smoothly here.

As Anthony removed his cloak, he added, "I'm sorry you don't have a private room. Shall I have a dressing screen brought up?"

Emma made a face. "Everyone in the household would know, and since we're just wed, speculation would be rampant. We'll manage well enough."

She went to the window, where a Christmas candle burned inside a special fixture designed to protect against fire. Every afternoon during the holiday season, a servant came around to clean the fixture and put in another candle that was designed to burn until dawn in a custom that was centuries old. Musingly Emma said, "I like being so high. When I was little, I would climb out on the roof and scamper around."

"In December?" His brows arched with surprise. "You were an intrepid little thing. Roof walking can be danger-ous, especially when it's icy."

"I only went out during mild weather, and I stopped entirely when my mother found out and made me promise not to do it again." Gazing out at the dark land-scape, she said dreamily, "I used to imagine flying off the roof and soaring over the hills."

Anthony had an unsettling image of her lying broken and lifeless in the wintry courtyard far below, her dark hair fanned about her and a glaze of ice crystals on her face. "I'm heartily glad that you never actually tried to fly."

"I've always had a firm grasp on the difference between dreams and reality. At least, I did as a child." She turned back toward the room. "I'd forgotten how women always flutter around you. Do you ever tire of it?"

He almost passed the comment off with a light reply. But the subject was one that should not be dismissed. "I suppose women like me because I like them. I'm not particularly flirtatious, you know."

She sighed. "I know. Just as flowers cannot help attracting honeybees, you can't help attracting females."

He'd always been grateful for that quality, but he understood that Emma might be less than enthused by the effects. "I can't stop them from buzzing, but you are my wife, Emma," he said seriously. "My one and only."

She nodded and spoke no more on the subject, but he sensed a certain sadness in her. He hoped that she wasn't beginning to regret her hasty marriage. He would have to try harder to make sure that she didn't.

A raucous bell clamored through the building. Even with a closed door between them and the source of the sound, it made a shocking amount of noise. Emma jumped and Anthony winced. "The fifteen minute bell. Since it will take us easily five minutes to walk to the salon, that gives us only ten minutes to get ready."

Emma frowned and went to the wardrobe. "Even though the duchess said this wouldn't be formal, I'll feel better if I put on something fresh." She took out a green gown. "Heaven only knows where Becky is. Could you help me with this, please?"

"Of course." Anthony came up behind her and began unfastening the complicated tapes and buttons of her traveling dress. When he was finished, he slid the garment down her arms. He swallowed hard when he saw the creamy slope of her shoulders. She had the most deliciously touchable skin he'd ever seen. It cried out for caresses.

Emma stepped out of the travel dress. Her shift and stays and petticoat covered as much of her as most gowns would, but there was a wicked sense of intimacy in seeing her in her unmentionables. He remembered what Madame Chloe had said about Emma's figure: *magnifique.* The modiste had been right. Emma was no fashionable sylph, but a woman of lush, sensual curves. He wondered how the weight of her full breasts would feel in his hands. A stab of swift heat ran through him.

Struggling to suppress that response, he went to the dressing table where Hawkins had laid out his brushes and other personal items. If there were more time, he would have shaved. Luckily, his chin was still presentable, though only just.

"I need help again." Emma had pulled on the gown, but could not manage the fastening herself.

Silently Anthony moved behind her again. His imagination was rioting. He wanted to lock the door and miss dinner and seduce his wife. But that really was not possible tonight, when they were both making a kind of homecoming.

Fingers uncharacteristically clumsy, he began tying the tapes. She'd put on a perfume with a complex, provocative scent. Not for her the girlish, floral fragrances.

His fingers brushed Emma's back as he tied a hidden bow. A little shiver went through her. Hoping it was shiver of pleasure, he leaned forward and kissed the juncture of her shoulder and throat. Her skin was silky warm under his lips. He wanted to lick her from head to toe. He settled for tracing the elegant curve of her ear with his tongue. Emma stiffened.

Though he'd had his fair share of female companionship, he wasn't such a coxcomb as to believe that he could infallibly sense what a woman wanted. And understanding this one was more important than any of his casual affairs. "Whenever I touch you, you seem to pull away," he said softly. "Would you rather I stopped?"

"No," she replied, her voice constricted. "I don't dislike your touch at all." She swallowed, her throat going taut. "Quite...quite the contrary."

Thank heaven for that! With the lightest of touches, he put his arms around her and cupped her breasts. She gasped, and he felt the hammering of her heart under his hands. Then, very gently, she leaned back against him in a silent gesture of trust and surrender. Her warm curves fitted against him as perfectly as matched puzzle pieces.

His own heart hammering, he said with deep feeling, "I really, really wish we didn't have to go down to dinner."

She turned her head and glanced up at him with an expression in her eyes as old as Eve. "We'll be back here later, and all the more eager for having waited."

He chuckled. "You've the makings of a wicked wench."

"Good," she said with great satisfaction.

Moving away from him with obvious reluctance, she went to finish her toilette. Anthony combed his hair rather blindly, since most of his attention was on the vivid memory of Emma in his arms. There was a gentle sensuality about her that made him simultaneously want to protect her and ravish her. Was this what marriage was about? Please God, he'd learn soon enough.

"I'm ready," Emma said with a touch of nervousness. "Do I look all right?"

He turned and surveyed her from head to foot. The shade of green she wore did wonderful things for her creamy skin and made her changeable eyes into a striking light green. Her softly waved chestnut hair was also far more flattering than the severe style she'd worn when they met. "You look perfect. Not too formal for tonight, but every inch a lady." He walked toward her. "There's only one problem."

Her expression, which had brightened, became anxious again. "What's wrong?"

"This." Women often wore gauzy scarves tucked around their necks as a way of making low-cut gowns more modest, and adding a bit of warmth as well. Emma had donned such a scarf. He swept it away, exposing the dramatic swell of her upper breasts. "You won't need this. With so many people present tonight, the rooms will be warm."

She blushed scarlet and instinctively brought her

hands up to cover her bare flesh. Dropping them again, she said apologetically, "I feel very bare."

"I've a cure for that." He went to his dressing case and pulled out a worn velvet box. Inside was a triple rope of pearls and a pair of matching earrings. "Not too many heirlooms survived my father's debts, but these did. They were my mother's, and now they are yours. Merry Christmas, Emma."

Emma caught her breath. "My mother had a necklace much like this, but hers had to be sold." A glint of tears in her eyes, she lifted the necklace and pressed it to her cheek. "Pearls have such a wonderful feel. Silky. Almost alive."

"They must be worn to be at their best." He took the necklace from her and clasped it around her neck. It was a lovely neck, long and graceful. He kissed the nape under her upswept hair. She made a small, breathy sound, and this time he knew that it was not distress.

Fingers not quite steady, Emma put on the earrings, then turned for his inspection. He said with absolute conviction, "You look lovely, Emma. Any man would be proud to have you by his side."

She gave him a smile so radiant that for a moment she took his breath his way. "I'm very glad you think so."

He offered his arm with a courtly bow, and together they went to rejoin their family.

CHAPTER 6

BUBBLING WITH ANTICIPATION, Emma held Anthony's arm as they went down the icy halls and staircases. He wanted her! Even an innocent could recognize the desire in his voice and his touch. He hadn't been uninterested before, merely giving her the period of adjustment that she'd requested.

Well, she was ready to be a wife now. In fact, she was eager for this long-awaited evening to be over so they could return to their room, and the waiting bed.

The thought made her glance up shyly. He met her gaze, and gave her an intimate smile. *His one and only*. The knowledge made her want to turn somersaults the way she had when in the nursery.

Almost floating, she let him guide her toward the main salon, where the adults were meeting for pre-dinner sherry. The great house looked exactly as she remembered, with the scent of pine boughs and the bright colors of holly berries and scarlet ribbons everywhere. Christmas at Harley was magical.

The salon was already teeming with people and noisy with talk when they entered. Emma looked around, trying to put names to faces. Most were cousins of some sort, though older family members had generally been made honorary aunts and uncles. Heavens, Aunt Agatha had put on weight. Lord only knew who that tall youth was, except that he was obviously a Vaughn. And was that young woman in blue her cousin Margaret, or could it be Margaret's sister, Mary?

Someone called out happily, "Verlaine has arrived!"

Emma smiled a little wryly, knowing it would be like this for the rest of their lives. It was Anthony whom people would remember, Anthony who would bring that smile to their faces. He had the same effect on her. As long as he was hers, she didn't mind sharing his attention at gatherings such as these.

People crowded forward to offer hugs and best wishes on their marriage. Emma knew she must be glowing like a Christmas candle. She'd dreamed of this warm welcome for ten years, and never believed she would feel it again. Once more she was a Vaughn among Vaughns. And to judge by the admiration in men's eyes, Anthony had not been lying when he said that she looked well.

The dowager duchess entered the room through another door, and many of the group around Emma and Anthony went to greet her. The dowager had been a great beauty as a girl, and she still was.

As the crowd thinned, Emma saw a young woman

standing by the great fireplace, her gaze turned in their direction. Emma caught her breath with surprise. It was Cecilia, and she hadn't changed at all. She must be near thirty, but even after two children, she was slim and graceful. As beautiful as she had always been.

Taking leave of the ancient aunt with whom she had been speaking, Cecilia came to greet the newcomers, her golden hair shining in the light of dozens of candles. Coming to a stop, she said, "It's wonderful to see you again, Emma. I'm so glad you're here."

The warmth in her voice seemed sincere; Cecilia had always been very pleasant to Emma. It wasn't her fault that her petite blond beauty made Emma feel like a great graceless ox by comparison. Barely managing a smile, Emma said, "Thank you, Cecilia. You look marvelous. Do your children favor you or Brand?"

"They are unmistakably Vaughns." Cecilia's face tightened and she turned to offer Anthony her hand. "Verlaine. It's been a long time since you've come to Harley."

"Cecilia." Anthony bowed over her hand, then straightened, still holding it. "It's...it's good to be here again." The tension between him and Cecilia was palpable.

Emma felt as if she'd been struck a physical blow. Of course there would be some reaction when two people who had once been sweethearts met again, but she had not expected Anthony to turn to marble. Blast it, she thought he'd put his feelings for Cecilia behind him! Instead, he was gaping like a moon calf.

The two were still gazing at each other as if they were

alone in the room. Feeling invisible, Emma released Anthony's left arm. He didn't even notice.

The moment stretched for a painful eternity. Then a tall, dark-haired man who looked like a slightly smaller version of Anthony materialized by Cecilia's side. It was Brand, looking as if he wanted to do murder. Taking his wife's arm, he said in a low, bitter voice, "Since this is my father's house, I cannot ask you to leave, or even cut you, Verlaine. But do not expect civility."

Anthony tore his gaze away from Cecilia and looked at his former friend. Visibly struggling to collect himself, he said, "I had hoped we would be able to make peace, Brand. I behaved badly the last time I was here, and you have my most sincere apology." He extended his hand tentatively.

His cousin looked as if he wanted to cut it off. "I'd rather invite the Great Plague to dinner than take your hand, Verlaine." He pivoted and stalked off, taking Cecilia with him. She cast a last miserable look over her shoulder, then went obediently.

Unable to face Anthony, Emma also spun away. She walked rather blindly through the room until she almost ran into an elderly man, Lord Edward Vaughn, the present duke's uncle.

"Emma, my dear child, how lovely to see you," he said jovially. Taking her hand, he drew her under a beribboned kissing bough that hung in the arch that divided the salon into two parts. Every open arch in Harley had a similar kissing bough. After a swift peck on the cheek, he said with twinkling eyes, "One of the advantages of being an old man is that I can now kiss all the pretty girls and my wife won't have my head for it."

Laughing, she said, "You're not that old, Uncle Edward. Not even seventy, and looking ten years younger." All of the Vaughns aged well; in another forty years, Anthony would look very like Lord Edward. Thinking of Anthony sent a pang through her. With a determined smile, she said, "Where is Lady Edward? I haven't seen her yet."

"Charlotte sent me to get you." Taking Emma's arm, he escorted her to a corner where his round, cheerful-looking wife was relaxing on a sofa. "Doesn't get around as well as she did, but she can still ask questions!"

Gratefully Emma sank down beside Lady Edward and prepared for a good-natured interrogation. At least it would keep her from thinking about Anthony, and his reunion with the divinely beautiful Cecilia.

AFTER BRAND TOWED CECILIA AWAY, Anthony took a deep, slow breath, startled at the turmoil of his own feelings. He thought he'd gotten over Cecilia years before. After all, she'd dropped him like a hot coal once received got a better offer. Yet seeing her had knocked him heels over head. He'd forgotten the impact of her beauty.

Yearning for Emma's good sense, he looked around and couldn't find her. Damnation, what must she be thinking? He had a fair idea, and the thought was not pleasant. He was about to start searching in earnest when the dinner bell rang. The dowager duchess appeared beside him with feline suddenness. She even had the sleekness and composure of a small, silver hair-haired cat. "You shall take me into dinner, Verlaine, and then sit beside me," she announced.

One did not refuse an order from the Dowager Duchess of Warrington. He offered his arm. "It will be my honor, Grandmére. I haven't seen you in far too long."

Not that she was his grandmother, but every Vaughn under the age of fifty called her that. As he led the dowager into the dining room, his heart gave a painful twinge. If he could not make peace with Brand this Christmas, he would be unable to return. A gentleman did not make another man uncomfortable in the man's own home. Aloud, he said, "Where do you wish to sit, Grandmére?"

She gestured. "Here, at the foot of the table."

Anthony pulled out her chair, then took the right hand seat. The long table was set for at least fifty people, he guessed.

The dowager explained, "The rest of the year, Amelia takes her place at this end as a proper duchess should, but tonight, since we dine informally, she can actually sit by her husband."

Sure enough, the duke was taking his seat at the far end of the table and his wife was next to him. They both had mischievous expressions from flouting convention. Breaking the rules was part of the holiday fun.

"I'm glad to see that you're finally settling down,

Verlaine," the dowager said in a low voice meant only for his ears. "I had begun to despair of you."

"I see you haven't lost your taste for assault, Grand-mére," he said pleasantly.

"At my age, there isn't enough time to waste it on social inanities." She regarded him unblinkingly, her pale blue eyes like aquamarine. "I was particularly pleased to hear that you'd married Emma Stone. You need a wife like her, with a brain in her head and a steady disposition."

"Happy though I am to be here, I'm beginning to remember the drawbacks of attending gatherings with people who have known one since the nursery," he said dryly.

She laughed. "Everyone knows your business, and has opinions on how you should run your life. It's part of belonging to a family, Verlaine." Her expression sobered. "I've been worried that you might go the same way as your father. You're very like him, you know. Charming, handsome, everything comes to you easily. Too easily. He never grew up, and the same could happen to you."

"I can't say that I appreciate the comparison," he said coolly. "My father was an irresponsible care-for-nobody who very nearly lost the family patrimony."

"It's a man's duty to care for his inheritance and pass it on to his children, and he failed badly in that," she agreed. "But from the tales I've heard of your gambling and wenching, your behavior has not been any better. I trust that you now intend to start behaving like an adult."

Having delivered that blow with the expertise of a

prizefighter, she turned to the man on her left. Anthony clamped down on his irritation. As soon as his father had died and the state of the Verlaine finances was revealed, Anthony had retrenched and done everything he could to save the estate. But it was also true that until that appalling day, he'd lived extravagantly, as if his income was drawn from a bottomless well.

For the life of him, he couldn't still couldn't think of any method other than gambling that he might have used to earn the money to redeem the mortgages. One certainly could not borrow such a sum from a friend, the banks had refused him, and he had not wished to turn fortune hunter. So he'd gambled, saving his winnings, never allowing wagering fever to overcome good sense, never spending money needlessly.

Yet in the end, gambling hadn't been enough. He would have lost Canfield if not for Emma. Most of the damage had been done by his father, but Anthony would have born the blame in the eyes of the world, just as he would have had to live with the consequences of his father's selfishness and waste. For two years, that bitter knowledge had eaten at him like acid. When he had a son, he'd do better by the boy.

It was the first time he'd seriously thought about having children, and he was surprised at the complicated emotions that accompanied the idea. Children, and Emma would be their mother. Her blood would flow in their veins, as would his.

It was one of the most obvious facts in the world, yet he had never really thought about it with respect to himself. Lord, what could a man do for his children that was more important than choosing a good mother for them? And Emma would be good—he knew that without question. Kind, patient, and intelligent, not to mention healthy and with a wry sense of humor that he was appreciating more and more.

Automatically he looked for her. She was sitting near the far end of the table, smiling at some comment made by her dinner partner. Anthony's mouth tightened. Perhaps he shouldn't have removed her neck scarf—the fellow was leering down her bodice as if she was the next dinner course.

Jealousy was also a new experience, one he didn't like. He'd never felt jealous of his mistresses. If they fancied another man, he'd always let them go cheerfully. But Emma was his *wife*. He found, rather uncomfortably, how much difference that made.

Luckily the woman on his right was exchanging a year's worth of news with her other neighbor, which relieved Anthony of the obligation to talk. He toyed with his leek soup and thought about what the dowager had said. *Charming, handsome, everything comes to you easily.* Emma and her fortune had certainly come easily.

As he sipped his wine, he wondered about that stroke of luck. Would she have found him and suggested marriage if he'd been ugly? What a sobering thought. He'd always known that beauty gave a woman power, while taking for granted the advantages that his own face and athletic form gave him.

Yet he could no more take credit for his looks than

for his title and station in life. His appearance was pure Vaughn, and the Verlaine title and fortune had been granted to the naval grandfather who'd been a famous admiral until his heroic death in battle.

By comparison, Anthony was forced to admit that he was basically a worthless fellow. He had spent his life pursuing pleasure. His father's death had sobered him, and his desire to save Canfield had given him a worthy goal, but he had still essentially been living the life of a heedless young man about town.

I've been worried that you might go the same way as your father. You're very like him, you know...He never grew up, and the same could happen to you...I trust that you mean to start behaving like an adult.

His gaze went to Emma again. Perhaps being an adult was a matter of letting go outgrowing the youthful belief that the world was a place of infinite possibilities. Not everything was possible. Every choice eliminated a myriad of other paths.

By marrying Emma, he had forfeited the right to take to wife any of London's dazzling beauties, just as she had given up the chance of marrying a man who might be more clever or worthy than Anthony. Since they had chosen each other, it was up to them to make their marriage closer to heaven than to hell.

With a wry smile, he realized that that was probably a very adult thought.

DETERMINED TO ENJOY THE EVENING, Emma managed to shut away the memory of that horrible moment between Anthony and Cecilia. She laughed her way through dinner with a cousin by marriage she'd never met. Afterward, as the men sat over their port, she made the rounds of her female relatives, exchanging hugs and news.

After the men joined the ladies, an impromptu concert began. Three young female cousins began singing carols while another played the pianoforte. Soon the instrument was surrounded by Vaughns who joined in. Emma did her share of singing, her heart aching a little as she watched some of the older couples. Lord Edward and his wife sat on a sofa, his arm around her waist. The duke and duchess were discreetly holding hands as they joined in the carols.

Would Emma and Anthony have that fondness for each other when twenty or thirty years had passed? Or would they be like Brand and Cecilia, who stood side by side with frozen faces, neither touching nor looking at one another?

Depressed by the thought that the odds were against her and her husband developing a long-term affection, Emma slipped away while the party was still going strong. No one would miss her, least of all Anthony, who was spreading his charm lavishly about the gathering.

She made the long climb to the tower room through silent passages. It was a welcome surprise to find a small fire burning when she arrived. The Harley coal bill for this fortnight would be astronomical.

After changing to her heaviest nightgown and a matching robe that went over it, she sat down at the dressing table and pulled the pins from her hair. As she was lifting her brush, the door opened and Anthony entered.

Their gazes met in the mirror. Voice carefully neutral, she said, "I thought you would be downstairs longer."

He closed the door and leaned back against it. "I made my excuses when I saw you leave. It took me a few minutes to break away, or I would have escorted you up."

She wondered if he'd come because of the sensual promise that had been between them when they dressed for dinner. Unfortunately, she was no longer in the mood to consummate her marriage even though Anthony looked almost irresistible. Tall and broad-shouldered, with dark hair waving over his forehead and his piercing eyes, he was a man too splendid to be the husband of Emma Stone. He was any young girl's dream. He'd been her dream.

She began brushing out her hair. Deciding that it was time for an inane comment, she said, "It was lovely to see everyone again."

"You're wondering about Cecilia," he said quietly.

She had not expected him to broach such a delicate subject. "As a matter of fact, I am." Looking in the mirror rather than at his face made it easier for her to ask, "Are you still in love with her?"

He hesitated. "No. At least, I don't think so. But seeing her again was a shock. It brought back what it felt like to be twenty." His mouth twisted. "I'd forgotten how wretched a time that was."

She turned to look at him directly. He was doing his best to be honest with her, and for that she was grateful. But she was not very reassured by the fact that he "didn't think" he was in love with Cecilia. "Brand looked as if he wanted to do murder."

"I really don't know why, since he got what he wanted —Cecilia. He hardly has cause to be jealous when I haven't laid eyes on her in nine years." Anthony sighed. "I always thought of him as having an easy disposition. Perhaps I didn't know him as well as I thought. There is a lot I didn't know."

Emma suspected that when a woman came between two men, the emotional equation could change dramatically. Certainly Brand appeared to have changed from the young man she remembered. But what did she know? She was just an aging spinster who had bought herself a husband. She began to braid her hair. "Perhaps when Brand gets over the shock of having you here, his mood will moderate."

"Perhaps," Anthony said, clearly unconvinced.

Emma tied the end of her braid, then rose and went to the bed. Outside scattered flakes of snow were falling. She hoped they would continue. She'd always love the beauty and silence of new snow. After taking off her robe and laying it over a chair, she slid under the covers.

His voice as neutral as hers, Anthony said, "Can you spare a blanket? I'll make up a bed on the floor."

It would be much easier if he wasn't near her, but she

couldn't be so selfish. "You'll freeze on the floor," she said in her most practical, governessy voice. "The bed is quite large enough for two." Then she rolled onto her side away from him, pulling the blankets protectively around her in an unmistakable sign that she would not welcome any amorous overtures.

She heard the rustling sounds of undressing. Before dinner, she would have peeked so she could admire him. Not now.

He put out all the candles except the one in the window, which had a tin reflector that sent most of the light outdoors. Then the mattress sagged as he lay down.

Though he didn't touch her, she was acutely aware of his nearness. Her husband. It was entirely within her rights to roll over and cuddle up against him. Perhaps he would draw her close and tell her how lovely she was, and how he was much happier to be with her rather than Cecilia...

She shouldn't have thought of Cecilia. Now the image of her husband and the woman he had loved was burning in her brain. He had never looked at Emma like that. With brutal honesty, she recognized that he probably never would.

It had been a mistake to try to build a new marriage at Harley. They were surrounded by too many ghosts, not all of whom were dead.

Swallowing hard against the painful lump in her throat, Emma closed her eyes and ordered herself to sleep.

CHAPTER 7

HOURS PASSED and Anthony's breathing had long since become slow and regular, but Emma still couldn't sleep. Never having shared a bed with a man in her life, she was painfully conscious that Anthony's warm, very male body was mere inches away. With half her mind on him and the other spinning ever more depressing visions of what her marriage might be like, sleep was impossible.

Finally, with an exasperated sigh, she slipped from the bed. The room was chilly, so she quietly put another scoop of coal on the fire. Then she went to the window. The light snow had intensified into huge soft flakes floating thickly through the windless air, covering the world with a pristine white mantle.

Unable to resist, she detached the Christmas candle fixture from the sill and set it aside. Then she opened the casement window and leaned out. The air was fresh and pure and stimulating, cold but not unpleasantly so. She inhaled deeply, feeling refreshed.

An outrageous idea struck her. She'd always loved both snow and the roofs of Harley. Why not go out? The roof wasn't really dangerous in this area because a low decorative balustrade ran along the edge. Between the angled roof and the balustrade was a two-foot wide walkway. She could easily step down onto it and go exploring.

She glanced back at Anthony. Her husband was sleeping as if he'd been drugged. He'd never know that she was gone.

The idea of going outside seemed somehow right. Being a little outrageous would make her feel less like plain Emma Stone, and more like the dashing Lady Verlaine that she wanted to be.

She felt her way to the wardrobe and located her cloak and half boots. After sliding her feet into the latter, she tossed the cloak over her nightgown. Then she clambered out the window. The snow was three or four inches deep.

After loosely closing the swinging casements behind her, she set off along the narrow walkway, her cloak swirling around her ankles. The slanting roof was to her right and the vast open spaces of the night on her left. It was wonderfully quiet. The snowflakes caught and magnified the subtle light, turning it into a pearly, otherworldly glow. Her worries began to dissolve, leaving her with a sense of serenity.

After walking across the long straight central block, she came to an awkward corner where the east wing met the main building. Rather than risk scrambling across it, she folded down into the corner. The sheltered position gave her a splendid view of the snow-covered planes and angles of Harley. Seen from this perspective, the great house was strange and lovely. Haunting, in fact.

Alone in the night, she was able to relax in a way that had been impossible in the bedchamber. She thought about Harold Greaves, lying in a new grave beside his wife. Was the snow also falling over their resting place in London? Mr. Evans had said they were close as only a childless couple could be.

She closed her eyes and offered a prayer that Mr. Greaves had been reunited with his wife in some better place. Every day she made at least one such prayer. It seemed the least she could do. Strange how her life had been changed utterly by a man she would never meet.

She wrapped her cloak closer. The cold was slowly seeping into her, but she wasn't ready to go inside again. Later. For now, she would simply let her mind drift...

ANTHONY AWOKE when something banged hard nearby. The wind had blown open the casement windows and snow was swirling into the room. It took a moment longer to remember where he was. Harley. Emma. The tower room.

Where *was* Emma? Not beside him in the bed.

He sat up and scanned the room, but the faint light of the fire did not reveal her. He got from the bed and lit several candles. No Emma, yet the door was still latched from the inside, as he had left it. How could she have left?

His gaze went to the open window, and he stiffened. The Christmas candle had been removed from the sill. Oh, God, no. Earlier she had talked about her childhood fantasy of flying from the roof and soaring over the hills. She couldn't possibly have been so upset about his encounter with Cecilia that she would have jumped. Could she?

Cold with fear, he threw open the casements and looked down into the courtyard, terrified that he would see a broken body far below. He could see nothing unusual...but if she had jumped, the snow might have covered her by now.

His hands locked on the sill until his fingers whitened. If she had done something terrible because of him...may God have mercy on both their souls.

Then he noticed faint marks on the narrow walkway below the window. Footsteps, perhaps, though so full of snow as to be almost invisible. But why the devil would she be out on the roof in the middle of the night?

Rather than struggle with boots, he slipped his feet into a light pair of evening shoes. Then he threw his cloak over his nightshirt and climbed out onto the roof. The snow was about six inches deep, and the same rising wind that had blown the window open was causing clouds of icy crystals to drift and eddy around him.

Grimly he started walking. Under other circumstances, he might have enjoyed the unearthly beauty around him. Instead he moved along the slippery walkway as quickly as possible, his attention divided between his footing and the ground far below.

He was nearing panic when he finally found her huddled in a corner. In fact, he almost fell over her. An inch or more of feathery snow covered her cloak, making her almost invisible in the white night. She was so still he feared that she was dead.

Heart hammering, he dropped to his knees beside her. Lacy flakes coated her face and dusted her dark lashes. Taking her hands, he said urgently, "Emma! Emma, are you all right!"

Her hands were like ice. He began chafing one of them between his. "Emma, dammit, wake up!"

Her lashes fluttered open, and she stared blankly at him. Praise God, at least she was still alive. He said sharply, "Can you walk?"

She blinked at him, dazed. "Anthony?"

"Yes, it's me. What the devil are you doing out here in the middle of a snow storm?" He stood, then took both her hands and pulled her up. She didn't fall, quite, but she swayed badly. He caught her around the waist.

Her tall body sagged against him. "I...I think I fell asleep."

"Idiot," he said brusquely. Half carrying her, he started the long trek back. The walkway that was adequate for one was hazardous for two, especially covered with soft, sliding snow. He took the outside edge himself, keeping one hand on the top of the balustrade and the other arm locked around his wife.

The trip back seemed three times as long as the one

out. Emma moved stiffly, sometimes slipping on the soft snow. Once her feet went out from under her and they both almost went over the edge. She seemed unaware of how close they had come to death, but Anthony was sweating with strain by the time they reached the tower room.

Knowing this last bit was the most dangerous, he braced one foot against the balustrade, then scooped Emma up and maneuvered her through the window. After setting her on her feet inside, he climbed through himself and latched the window tight.

He dropped his cloak and kicked off his ruined shoes, then turned to his wife. Emma was shivering uncontrollably. He tossed aside her cloak and seated her in a chair by the fire. After throwing coal on lavishly, he brought a branch of candles close and examined her. Though she seemed barely aware of her surroundings, he couldn't find signs of frostbite on her face or hands or feet.

He hesitated, considering what to do. Putting her in a hot bath would probably warm her quickly, but finding servants to heat the water would take time. Too much time. Even locating brandy would take longer than he wanted. She needed to be warmed up immediately.

Actually, the best way to warm her was probably with his own body. He found a heavy pair of his socks and put them on her icy feet. Then he drew her upright. "It's back to bed, my girl."

He tugged her nightgown up over her head. She didn't resist, except for a faint squeak of protest.

Under other circumstances, he would have been

paused to admire the lush femininity of her body, but not this time. He tucked her into bed and pulled the blankets over her, adding the spare from the wardrobe. Then he snuffed all but one candle, stripped off his own garments, and slid under the covers.

Lying on his side, he drew her into his arms so that her spine and was pressed into his stomach and her bottom was against his groin. Damnation, but she was cold. He breathed warm air on the back of her ear and began rubbing the chilled length of her arm.

"What...what are you doing?" she said, sounding more aware.

"Trying to keep you from the death by freezing you so richly deserve." He slid his knee between her icy thighs.

She stiffened and tried to wriggle free, which only pressed her icy but shapely rump into him harder. He tightened his arm around her and began massaging her the cold curves of hip and thigh. "Hold still. The sooner you warm up, the less likely you are to come down with lung fever."

"Why...why didn't you just leave me out there?" she asked a little breathlessly.

"Because losing my wife after less than a fortnight of marriage would look like damned carelessness on my part," he retorted.

"It would have been worth a little gossip," she said hazily. "I have another forty five thousand pounds in trust for me and my children. If I died now, you'd inherit the lot."

His hand stilled. Christ, did she realize what she was

saying? "If I understand you correctly," he said acidly, "you didn't trust me enough to reveal the truth about your fortune, and you're now suggesting I should have murdered you for your money. Why the devil would you marry a man you find so contemptible?"

"Better the devil you know..." she muttered as she tried to writhe away again.

As he caught at her, his hand came down on her breast. The soft weight fit his hand perfectly. She inhaled sharply, and they both became very still.

He released her breast with reluctance. She may or may not be getting warmer, but he certainly was. "So I'm the devil you know. How flattering. Remind me to thrash you someday when the circumstances are more appropriate."

"You wouldn't dare!" she said indignantly, sounding more herself.

"I restrain myself only because my mother taught me never to strike a female, no matter how richly she deserves it." Though his voice was dryly humorous, he was uncomfortably aware that she would not have made her bizarre suggestion about leaving her to freeze if she didn't secretly fear that he didn't want to be married to her.

If she had died through no fault of his own, would he be relieved to be rich and free again? The answer in his head was an instant, vehement *No*. It was time to be an adult. To take on responsibility, to build a family. And if Emma was not the wife he would have chosen, she was the wife he had, and he was not displeased by that. Not displeased at all.

He began rubbing her again. She was noticeably warmer. As his concern receded, sexual awareness became impossible to suppress. He had a beautiful, naked female body in his arms, and she was his wife. Or almost.

He wanted, rather desperately, to make love to her. Yet on a level beyond arousal he sensed that this was a critical moment. What he did now would influence the rest of his life. He moved his hand from her side to the front of her body, stroking from magnificent breasts over curving torso down to her soft belly. Her skin was satin smooth and blessedly warm.

"Your view of my character is rather unflattering, and I can't say that I blame you for that," he said quietly. "I've been an irresponsible, frivolous fellow most of my life, and you and I married for mutual convenience, not love. But I assure you, Emma, I do take our marriage seriously."

He propped himself up on one elbow and looked down at her as he tried to shape what he wanted to say. "I will do my best to fulfill the vows I made on our wedding day, as I trust you to honor the ones you made to me. If we do that, perhaps in time love will come. If not love, surely we can manage caring and respect."

She rolled onto her back and looked at him. In the dim light of the single candle, her eyes were a smoky gray, and fully aware. Their gazes held for a long, long moment.

Then she raised her left hand and touched the side of his face with gentle fingers. "Caring and respect are easy, Anthony," she whispered. "You already have mine."

He did not deserve so much from her. Turning his head, he tenderly kissed the shiny new wedding band he'd slid onto her finger two weeks before. That, at least, he had bought with his own money. Softly he said, "With this ring I thee wed."

He laid her hand on the mattress. "With my body I thee worship." Then he leaned forward and kissed her. Her mouth was warm and soft and welcoming.

"As long as we both shall live," he said huskily as he moved his lips to her throat.

Her arms came around him hard, and once again they were flesh to flesh. But this embrace was not for warmth or consolation. It was wholly carnal as the desire in him sang to the sleeping desire in her.

Her response was hesitant at first, but as honest and true as Emma herself. He caressed her lavish, womanly body, searching for what pleased her, and discovered that everything did. Every touch, every kiss. Every gentle exploration, every discovery of a new, secret place.

Despite the urgency of his own craving, he took his time. It was very much in his best interest for her to be a joyous, ardent partner. The longer he denied himself now, the more unselfishly he wooed her, the greater the reward for them both.

He pleasured her until she gasped with wonder, her body convulsing and her arms locking desperately around him. Then, when her ragged breathing slowed, he claimed the final intimacy that made her his wife. At first she stiffened from the pain. Panting with the effort of restraint, he held still and soothed her with soft words and gentle kisses until she relaxed and began to rock against him.

Together they found a rhythm that went from mutual exploration to fierce possession to the final madness. And in the end, she cried out his name in a voice that pierced him to the heart.

They both collapsed, spent and shaking. He buried his face in her thick silky hair as he struggled for breath. How strange that he, who considered himself a master of the amatory arts, should have learned so much from her. His sweet, wise, brave wife.

As his breathing slowed, he rolled onto his side and drew her once again into his arms. Soon she was asleep, her head trustingly on his shoulder.

He stayed awake a little longer, drowsy but struck by the wonder of what had taken place between. Letting his hand rest in her tangled hair, he murmured, "My one and only." Then he, too, slid into sleep.

EMMA AWOKE the next morning to blue skies and pale wintry sunshine. The events of the previous night might have seemed a dream, except that Anthony slept beside her. He was gloriously naked, with one powerful arm wrapped around her waist to hold her close. She should be embarrassed at being equally naked, but her sense of well-being was too great. The sheer animal warmth of her position made her want to purr.

She was in love. What she had felt for Anthony when she was a girl had not been mere infatuation, but the first distant notes of what was now a grand symphony of emotions. Whatever the future held, that love would always be an integral part of her.

She lay in mindless contentment until she succumbed to the need to stretch. When she moved, Anthony's eyes opened. His dark lashes were really ridiculously long, a devastating frame for his light eyes.

His mouth curved into a smile. "Remember—any

more night walks on the roof in snowstorms, and you get thrashed."

"Yes, my lord and master," she said, her meek words belied by her saucy smile.

His hand moved lazily, possessively, to her breasts. "I'm going to like being married to you. I'm glad you were foolish enough to propose to me."

The desire to say that she loved him was almost overwhelming. Firmly she clamped down on it. This was not the right time for such a declaration; it might never be the right time. At least they had become friends. Not only had Anthony risked his life to rescue her from her own foolishness, but they had shared profound intimacy.

Some of her pleasure dimmed as she realized that for him, sexual relations must be a matter of course. Needing to know how he felt about what they had done, she said shyly, "Last night—is it always as nice as that?" She felt herself blushing. "The...the being married part, I mean."

His brows arched, and she could feel her heart sinking. Why had she assumed that he had taken any special pleasure in what she had found so rapturous?

"Nice?" he repeated in a deep, ominous voice. "We discover a rare degree of passion together, and all you can say is '*nice?*'"

Even as she recognized that he was teasing, she blushed some more. "Well, I have nothing to compare it to. I would appear foolish rhapsodizing over something that was utterly routine." She paused pensively. "Though if that was routine, no married person would ever get out of bed."

He laughed and caught her in his arms, rolling her over so that she was lying on top of him. "No, my sweet Emma. Last night was not routine by any standard. It was special." He kissed the tip of her nose. "As special as you are."

She didn't think it was possible for her to be any happier. Stretching out along his warm, muscular frame, she said softly, "I'm glad you think so."

He skimmed his hands slowly down her back and hips, stirring delicious sensations in places that she hadn't even known existed before the previous night. "Are you sore this morning?"

"Only a little. I'm not the least bit refined or delicate, you know. My mother once said that with all the riding and tree-climbing I did, I'd have an easy wedding night. She seems to have been right." Emma rocked her hips against his provocatively. "I'm certainly not sore enough to forgo what I think is about to happen."

"Delicacy is overrated," he said huskily. "Let's *not* get out of bed all day."

And he pulled her head down for a kiss.

THEY DID rise in time for a very late breakfast. In the cheerful confusion of the house party, they hadn't been missed. Emma was glad when Anthony suggested a walk after they'd eaten. Much as she loved socializing with her long-lost family, she wanted to savor the enthralling new intimacy between her and her husband.

The previous night's storm had transformed the landscape into white sculptured shapes of unearthly beauty. As the wind blew icy plumes from the drifts, they set off along a lane where no one else had walked.

The snow was about six inches deep, which made walking awkward, but Anthony helped Emma through the drifts and kissed her at every stile. When they reached the shelter of a beech wood, she gave into temptation and flopped on her back in a drift. "I'm going to make an angel," she said as she energetically waved her arms up and down through the soft snow. "I haven't done this since I was a child."

Anthony laughed and lay down beside her. "Neither have I. Why do we stop doing things like this when we grow up?"

She propped herself on one elbow and studied her husband's snow angel critically. Since he was unhampered by skirts and his cloak was less voluminous, his angel was better than hers. "I don't know, but perhaps that's one reason for having children. One can pretend to do childish things for their sakes, rather than for oneself."

She hesitated, then said awkwardly, "I should have told you about the other forty five thousand pounds. It wasn't that I didn't trust you, but..." Her voice trailed off. She *hadn't* trusted him. But she did now. "I'll tell Mr. Evans that I've changed my mind about putting the money in a trust."

Anthony said gravely, "The gesture is much appreciated, but it's not necessary. You had every right to protect your future from a man who might be irresponsible. In fact, based on my history, probably was." He reached out and took her gloved hand in his. "We don't need the money. Now that the mortgages are cleared, Canfield will give us a very comfortable living. Keep the trust for our children."

She squeezed his hand, loving the way he said "our children" so naturally. It was tacit acknowledgment of the fact that they were going to build a life together.

His expression became less serious. "We've done snow angels. Now it's time I taught you about snow devils."

Her brows drew together. "I've never heard of them."

A wicked light in his eyes, he stripped off his gloves and tossed them aside. "I should hope you haven't."

Then he pounced, trapping her with his body as his cloak fell around them both. As she gave a squeak of surprise, he captured her mouth in a mesmerizing kiss.

It was a wonder they didn't melt the snow.

ANTHONY and his wife finished a thoroughly decadent day by napping after their walk. When they rose and prepared for dinner, he wondered if his intrepid bride would have been as eager for another passionate session as she had been for the earlier ones. He'd been too drained to find out, but was sure that by the end of the evening, when they went to bed again, he would have recovered sufficiently to offer another example of husbandly devotion.

Smiling for no particular reason, he glanced at Emma, who was putting a pair of gold earrings he bought for her. Even though he'd always fancied petite blondes, he must admit that his wife, who was exactly the opposite, was quite irresistible. Even now, when desire was temporarily sated, he wanted her. It was impossible to imagine <u>not</u> wanting her, no matter how many years they were married.

The dinner bell jangled through the long halls. Emma rose from the dressing table and turned slowly. "Do I look all right?"

He found her lack of confidence rather endearing. "You look magnificent," he said with complete sincerity. "That shade of russet silk is perfect for your coloring." And this time she was not covering her bountiful curves with a gauze scarf.

She smiled and took his offered arm. "The only drawback to a formal dinner is that I can't sit next to you."

He said meaningfully, "That doesn't matter, since you'll sleep next to me."

Her blush was so enchanting that he paused to nibble from her ear to her shoulder. She tasted delicious. Both of them were breathing more quickly when he escorted her from the room. If it weren't for Brand's enmity, this would be a perfect holiday.

AFTER A LONG AND LAVISH DINNER, the duchess rose in the signal for the ladies to withdraw. As the crowd of women made their laughing way the drawing room, the dowager duchess appeared beside Emma. "Come, child. I want to talk to you. We've scarcely had a chance so far."

"So many Vaughns, so little time," Emma said with a laugh. "You're in such demand, Grandmére, that I didn't wish to monopolize you."

"Then I shall monopolize you instead," the dowager said tranquilly. In pale, ice-blue silk and ostrich plumes, she was as lovely now as in the portrait Gainsborough had painted when she was twenty and a newlywed duchess.

When they reached the drawing room, the dowager steered Emma to a pair of wing chairs set in a quiet corner. As they seated themselves, she said, "Is Verlaine treating you well?"

Emma blushed. "Very well, Grandmére. We have much still to learn about each other, but we...we seem to suit."

"I guessed as much,' the dowager said, her faded blue eyes twinkling, "when I saw you coming in from your walk this afternoon. Such a quantity of snow on you both."

Another blush. Really, Emma thought with resignation, she'd blushed more in the last few days than in the previous ten years.

"I'm so glad you married Verlaine," the dowager said seriously. "He has a good heart, but he needed an anchor, a sense of direction. You'll give that to him, I think."

Startled, Emma said, "I thought the benefits of this marriage went mostly to me."

"Not at all. A good marriage is a benefit to both partners," the dowager said briskly. "You will give Verlaine stability, and he will teach you to laugh and enjoy life."

Emma looked down at her wedding ring, absently turning it on her finger. "I haven't had many opportunities for laughter in the last ten years."

The dowager sighed. "I wish you had come here. Even if you wouldn't stay at Harley, surely we could have found better employment for you than what you had."

Emma glanced up. "You were responsible for the fact that every year I received a Christmas invitation, weren't you? That's how you know about my various employers."

The dowager nodded. "I was afraid you might be lost to us, so I did my best to ensure that wouldn't happen. You should have come long ago."

Emma had not known that anyone was so interested in the welfare of an orphan who was a mere connection, scarcely a member of the family at all. A little defensively, she said, "I wanted to be here, Grandmére, but I could not have left my work for so long. Nor could I have come as a beggar."

"You have your share of Vaughn pride," the dowager said dryly. "I know it well." Laying a gentle hand on Emma's, she continued in a softer voice, "But my dear girl, I want you to know that you would have always been welcome."

Emma swallowed hard, torn between tears and a strong desire to kick herself. The dowager was right—it was foolish pride that had kept her away, far more than her circumstances. Still, she was here now. She gave the dowager a heartfelt hug. It healed a loneliness deep inside to know that she never really stopped being a Vaughn.

WHEN THE DUKE of Warrington gave the signal that it was time to leave the port decanter, Anthony held back as the rest of the men—including Brand—got to their feet and ambled off to rejoin the ladies. In a group so large, it was proving fairly easy to avoid his glowering cousin.

It was a Harley custom to have casual dancing the evening before Christmas Eve. Anthony had always enjoyed the event more than the grand Twelfth Night ball that would end the house party. For some of the younger guests, this would be the first public dancing of their lives. That had been true for Anthony a dozen years earlier. He smiled at the thought of how grown up he had felt then, when in fact he'd been the merest boy.

He joined the stream of Vaughns heading toward the ballroom, where a pianoforte was playing seductively. Emma would have been too young to dance at Harley during her last visit. He looked forward to introducing his wife to the polished dance floor.

A small hand touched his arm. He turned and found Cecilia regarding him with great tragic eyes. "Anthony, I must talk to you," she said urgently. "In private."

He hesitated. "It would not look good for us to go off together."

"No one will notice." She touched his arm again, seeming on the verge of tears. "Please, Anthony."

He glanced around, but didn't see Brand. With so many people milling about, a brief absence would not be noted. "Very well, Cecilia," he said without enthusiasm. "Where shall we meet?"

She thought. "The gallery."

"You go ahead. I'll follow in a few minutes."

She nodded and headed down the passage that ran to the main hall. Anthony waited until she was out of sight, then followed at an unhurried pace. The gallery was a long chamber on the floor above. It served several purposes, from displaying paintings and fencing foils to providing a walking area in inclement weather.

When Anthony arrived, Cecilia was lighting more candles with a Christmas candle from one of the windows. She glanced up nervously at his entrance, then replaced her candle in its window fixture. In the soft light, she looked fragile and almost unbearably lovely, as petite and exquisite as a gilded marzipan holiday angel.

Wryly recognizing that he was not the kind of man who could stay angry with an attractive woman, Anthony said, "What did you wish to discuss with me, Cecilia? Is something wrong?"

She nodded, her eyes brimming with tears. "Will you talk to Brand? He has the absurd notion that you and I have been having an affair!"

"What!" Anthony stared at her, shocked. "Where did he get such a ridiculous notion?"

"I have no idea." Tears began spilling from Cecilia's

blue eyes. "Oh, Anthony, everything has gone wrong and I don't know what to do!"

According to Anthony's mother, it was a gentleman's duty to allow a lady to cry all over his best waistcoat if she was in distress. Recalling that Cecilia had always had a tendency toward melodrama, he put an arm around her soothingly. "Surely things aren't that bad, Cecy."

She clutched at him, weeping harder than ever.

Brand chose this inauspicious moment to enter the gallery. He stopped dead in the doorway, his face going dead-white. Then he strode forward, eyes blazing. "Damn you, Verlaine! I knew I'd find you with Cecilia in your arms."

"If so, you're cleverer than I," Anthony said with exasperation. "She's your wife, Brand. Let her cry over on your shoulder." He disentangled himself from Cecilia, hoping that would defuse a potentially volatile situation.

No such luck. Brand stalked over to the rack of fencing foils and grabbed two of the weapons. "Tonight I'm going to do what I should have done nine years ago." Grimly he flicked the protective buttons off the points of the foils, then tossed one of the weapons hilt first to Anthony. "I challenge you to a duel. Right now, right here."

"For God's sake, Brand!" Anthony exclaimed as he reflexively caught the foil. "It's bad form for you to challenge a guest, or for me to accept. For that matter, if you're the challenger, I get to choose the weapons, and I don't choose swords."

"We'll do it *now!*" Brand barked at he stripped off his close-fitting coat. *"En garde!"*

Beginning to feel seriously concerned, Anthony removed his own coat, keeping a wary eye on his angry cousin. "This is ridiculous. I'm damned if I know what I've ever done to make you determined to kill me."

"Oh, you most assuredly will be damned," Brand said in a voice like a whip. "Prepare yourself, Verlaine, because tonight justice will be mine."

Then, as Anthony stared in stunned disbelief, the man who had once been his best friend lunged at him with glittering blade and murderous eyes.

CHAPTER 9

AFTER HER AUDIENCE with the dowager duchess, Emma left the nearly empty drawing room to go to the ballroom. She was looking forward to her first waltz with Anthony. He undoubtedly a superb dancer. She was badly in need of practice, but she didn't think that would matter.

As she entered the hall that led to the ballroom, she saw Cecilia slip away from the crowd ahead and go down the cross passage that went to the foyer and the main staircase. Emma thought nothing of it, until she saw Anthony leave as well, and he was heading the same way as Cecilia.

Emma stopped in her tracks, her stomach turning. Surely Anthony could not be having an assignation with Cecilia, not after what had transpired between him and Emma last night and today!

She swallowed hard and told herself not to be a ninny. The fact that Anthony and Emma had gone off in the same direction was hardly proof of amorous intentions. In fact, they'd both looked rather tense, not at all like a couple in pursuit of illicit pleasures.

Fiercely she told herself that she must learn to trust her husband, or she would go mad, for there would always be women hovering around him. Nonetheless, not feeling ready to face the laughing people in the ballroom, she sank into a chair tucked beside a massive carved console table.

Until now, she had not let herself wonder if Anthony would be a faithful husband, because the answer was probably not one she would like. Many men of his class had mistresses, and a man who loved women as Anthony did was a prime candidate for infidelity. Her heart bled a little at the thought.

Would she still love her husband even if he was unfaithful? Probably—but if that ever happened, part of her would retreat from him. Never again would there be the openness and trust that had occurred today.

She sat very still and concentrated on her breathing until it was regular again. There. She had faced the worst. If Anthony was unfaithful, at least she would be a little prepared. *But please God, don't let it happen!*

She was about to continue to the ballroom when she saw Brand stalk out and head in the direction that Anthony and Cecilia had gone. His face was like granite. Merciful heaven, had he seen them leave? If he caught the two of them together, there would be hell to pay, even if the meeting was perfectly innocent.

Swiftly Emma considered what to do. Go for the

duke? He would certainly put a quick end to any conflict. But by the time she found him, it might be too late. Better to follow Brand and hope that she could head off any trouble.

She got to her feet and walked after Brand, her long legs covering the ground quickly. By the time she reached the great hall, he was disappearing from sight on the upper floor, heading toward the gallery. Emma followed, praying that she was being an absolute idiot and nothing untoward was going to happen.

Halfway up the stairs, she was halted in her tracks by a woman's scream. Merciful heavens, Cecilia! Lifting her skirts indecorously, Emma raced upward, knowing with icy certainty that years of festering anger had reached the explosion point.

THOUGH ANTHONY'S mind was stunned by Brand's attack, years of fencing practice saved him. As Cecilia shrieked, Anthony knocked aside his cousin's blade. Retreating, he exclaimed, "Christ, Brand! Have you gone mad?"

"It's you who are mad, to meet my wife in my own house." Brand attacked again, this time controlled and far more dangerous than in his initial lunge.

With a shriek of clashing steel, Anthony countered well enough to save himself from injury, but this couldn't last long. Brand had always been a better swordsman, and now he was in a blind rage.

Hearing the door open, Anthony spared a swift glance, hoping to see the duke or one of the duchesses. They were the only people Brand might heed. Instead, Emma entered. Christ, she was the last person he wanted to see. If he was going to be spitted like a lamb for roasting, he did not want his wife to have to witness it.

In the instant that his attention was divided, Brand drove in again, slashing at his opponent's sword arm. Anthony managed to block his cousin's blade, but only just. The sleeve of his shirt was ripped from elbow to wrist. Knowing he could not retreat forever, Anthony stood his ground, fighting back furiously. He managed to battle Brand to a standstill as their blades shrilled together with metallic fury.

Then heavy folds of fabric whipped violently between them, trapping the foils and knocking them downward. With amazement, Anthony saw that Emma had wrenched one of the great tapestries from the wall and slammed it over the dueling weapons. She looked like a furious Valkyrie.

"Bloody hell!" Brand sneezed from the dust released by the tapestry. "For God's sake, Emma, stay out of this, or you'll get hurt."

Not moving, Emma snapped, "What the devil is this all about?"

"It's none of your affair." Recovering from the shock, Brand wrenched his weapon free from the heavy fabric and prepared to resume fighting.

"None of my affair when you're trying to kill my

husband?" she exclaimed. "Men! Of course this is my affair."

Deciding it was time to take a hand, Anthony hurled his foil away. The sword flew across the gallery and stabbed into the wall about a yard above the floor, then hung there, quivering. "Enough, Brand! I won't fight you any more, not when I haven't the faintest idea why you're so outraged."

For a terrifying moment, it appeared as if Brand might renounce a lifetime of gentlemanly training and attack an unarmed man. Then Emma grabbed the cowering Cecilia's hand. "Come on, Cecy, make yourself useful."

She hauled her smaller cousin between the men so that the two women formed a barrier. Then, with a practiced schoolteacher voice, she ordered, "Brand, explain yourself."

He looked mulish, which at least was an improvement over homicidal. Since he seemed unwilling to speak, Anthony said helpfully, "From what Cecilia told me, Brand suspects me of having an affair with her."

Emma's face tightened, but her voice was calm when she asked, "Are you?"

"Don't be absurd!" he retorted. "Until yesterday, I hadn't laid eyes on Cecilia in nine years."

Emma turned to Brand. "You heard what Anthony said. Do you honestly think they're having an affair?"

Brand wiped his brow with one forearm. Though he still looked dangerous, the wildness had faded from his eyes. "There might not be a physical affair," he admitted gruffly. "But Anthony has stood between Cecy and me every day and night of our marriage. When he fought me after she accepted my proposal, he said..." Brand stopped and swallowed hard. "He said that whenever I bedded my wife, she would be thinking of him. And he was right, damn him."

Cecilia gasped. "Brand, how can you say that? I could have married Anthony if I wanted to, but I chose *you*. What made you think I secretly preferred Anthony?"

"Everyone always did!" Brand stared at his wife, his expression anguished. "He was always the leader. Smarter, more charming, more handsome, everyone's darling—including yours. You only married me because I have a greater fortune and title."

Anthony cringed as he remembered how he'd flung both those taunts in Brand's face when they'd fought over Cecilia. Who would have believed that his angry words would have taken such poisonous root?

Exasperated, Emma said, "Don't you two ever *talk* to each other?" She unobtrusively removed Brand's foil from his relaxed grip. "Cecilia, why did you marry Brand instead of Anthony? I'm sure you had your reasons."

"I married him because I loved him, of course." She hesitated, then said painfully, "I loved them both, really, even though they're so different. But I'd always thought that Brand's feelings for me were more those of a brother. Anthony was the one who treated me like a sweetheart. He and I drifted into thinking that we would marry, even though he hadn't formally offered."

By this time, tears were running down Cecilia's

cheeks. Emma wordlessly produced a handkerchief from somewhere and handed it over. After Cecilia had blotted her eyes and blown her adorable little nose, she continued, "Then Brand asked me to be his wife, and I realized instantly that he was the husband I wanted, not Anthony." She stared at Brand beseechingly. "Do you remember what happened after I accepted?"

Her husband turned an interesting shade of red. "Of course I remember," he said stiffly. "But that is hardly something to be discussed before others!"

Blushing herself, Cecilia gave a nod of agreement. "I didn't accept because of your fortune or your title, though of course I didn't object to becoming a duchess. But what I loved was your...your steadiness. The way you made me feel cherished. Special." She gave Anthony an apologetic glance. "Marrying Anthony would have been very jolly, but he would always have mistresses and we might have ended up in debtors' prison. I didn't want that. I wanted *you.*"

Anthony felt a sharp pang at her words. She hadn't trusted him. It was not flattering knowledge. Yet he could not blame her for her mistrust. Emma hadn't entirely trusted him, either.

Brand swallowed hard, a muscle jumping in his throat as he stared at his wife. "I...I wasn't second best?"

"Never!" Cecilia's tears began flowing again. "But after we married, I began to wonder if you'd ever really loved me. As time went on and you became colder and colder, I...I decided that you had only wanted me because Anthony did. You two were always competing, and I was

merely one more prize. Once you had me, you lost interest."

Anthony winced. He couldn't speak for Brand, but he had to admit that there had been an element of competition in his courtship of Cecilia. She'd been the prettiest girl around, so he had assumed that he, dashing Anthony, everyone's darling, deserved her.

Sometimes he didn't like himself very much.

Speaking as if he and his wife were alone, Brand said hoarsely, "How could you think that, Cecy? You're the only woman I've ever loved. But you never said that you loved me, not once."

"You never said that you loved me, either," she said starkly.

"At first it seemed unnecessary," he said painfully. "Later, I couldn't because I started thinking that you had married me for the wrong reasons. It was like...like acid in my belly."

Cecilia went into his arms, sobbing, "Oh, Brand, Brand! Why didn't we talk like this years ago? I've always loved you, even when I was sure that you didn't love me."

Brand embraced his wife with feverish intensity, his own eyes glittering with tears. They clung together for a long moment. Then he looked up and said haltingly, "Anthony, I'm sorry. I've behaved abominably. I wanted to blame you for wrecking my marriage, because that was easier than blaming myself. Can you forgive me?"

Anthony realized that he was being given a golden opportunity to act like an adult. "Much of the fault was mine, Brand. I didn't want to believe that Cecilia preferred you, so I said things no man should ever say to another. I'm sorry." He offered his hand.

Brand reached out and grasped it fervently. With surprising pleasure, Anthony realized that once again they could be friends. If the truth be known, he'd missed Brand far more than he'd missed Cecilia.

Emma, who had been watching approvingly, made a small movement of her head toward the door. Understanding, Anthony ended the handshake. "Can you forgive me, too, Cecilia? I never meant to injure your marriage."

She gave him a teary smile. "Brand and I did most of the damage ourselves. From now on we'll do better, won't we, dearest?"

"We will, darling. I swear it!" Brand bent his head and kissed his wife passionately, one hand slipping down her back to pull her hard against him. The air crackled with sexual tension.

Knowing they would not be missed, Anthony collected his coat. Then he and Emma quietly left the gallery. "I'd forgotten what a watering pot Cecilia is," he murmured when he'd closed the door behind them. "Thank heaven you're not like that."

After donning his coat and straightening his cravat, he draped his left arm around his wife's shoulders and they made their way down the stairs. "That was a very timely intervention, my dear," he said sternly. "But don't you *ever* put yourself between two armed men again, or I'll have to thrash you. You could have been killed."

She said demurely, "If every day you forbid me from

doing another thing on pain of being thrashed, very soon I'll be restricted to sitting by the fire with a book."

He smiled, but it quickly faded. "Who would have thought that the angry words I yelled at Brand nine years ago could have such terrible, lasting effects? I almost ruined his marriage. I swear before God, Emma, I never meant for that to happen."

"Words have power, Anthony," she said quietly. "Especially angry words thrown by someone like you, who affects people so strongly."

Everything comes to you easily. Too easily. "If I have power, I've used it badly," he said with self-disgust. "I've lived my life on the surface, sliding from one thing to another with never a serious thought in my head."

"That's probably true," Emma said with a depressing amount of objectivity. "But as Cecilia said, they did most of the damage to themselves. If either of them had had the courage to admit their love, they could have saved themselves years of misery."

"Perhaps in the long run their marriage will be better for having been tested like that. I hope so."

"You have also used your power of words for good, you know," Emma said quietly. "I think I remember every friendly word you ever said to me when I was a child. And there were many, even though you couldn't have been particularly interested in a plain, shy girl years your junior."

"Was I kind, Emma? I hope so." He smiled ruefully. "I have to admit that I don't remember that much about our encounters. You were merely one of many smaller Vaughns."

They'd come to an archway that divided two halls. A kissing bough hung there, so he stopped and turned Emma to face him. As he studied the strong, well-shaped planes of her face, the intelligence and warmth in her eyes, he wondered how he ever could have thought her plain. "I don't want us to become like Brand and Cecilia, hurting each other by not saying what we mean." He grinned. "Luckily, as alarmingly honest as you are, I don't think that will be a problem."

Her gaze dropped. "If I must be honest, then I shall have to admit that I've always loved you, Anthony, even when I was a child. When Mr. Evans mentioned that you were in desperate financial straights, I dismissed every other possibility and ran straight to you, hoping you were desperate enough to marry me." Her mouth twisted wryly. "Luckily, you were."

She looked up again. Her great eyes, more gray than green tonight, were regarding him without hope or illusion. She did not expect love, but she did deserve honesty.

What did he feel for this woman who was his wife? Respect, certainly. Desire absolutely. Liking and protectiveness and a hundred other things. In fact, he recognized with lightning bolt suddenness and power, he was in love with her. It was so obvious. So right. The passion and intimacy and laughter between them were the truest thing he'd ever found his life, entirely different from his boyish yearning for Cecilia.

It took a moment for him to collect his scattered thoughts. Then, his gaze holding hers, he said slowly, "I can't claim to have loved you most of my life, Emma, but rather to my own surprise, I seem to have fallen quite madly in love with you."

Holding her face between his hands as if she were made of rare, fragile porcelain, he kissed her, the first kiss of true love he'd ever given in his life. In it was tenderness and desire and a growing sense of awe. Emma kissed him back with a sweet intensity that brought her spirit closer to his than he would have dreamed possible.

After a long, long embrace, he lifted his lips a few inches and said huskily, "Yesterday the dowager said that things come easily to me, and she's right. Through no effort or virtue of my own, I've acquired the best of all possible wives."

He ran his admiring gaze over Emma's richly curved body. "It's something of a bonus that you're the most alluring woman I've ever known. What more could a man ask of the only woman he'll ever lie with again?"

She caught her breath. "Do you mean that, Anthony?"

Fidelity struck him as a very adult, very desirable trait. "I swear and vow, Emma, that you will be my one and only as long as we both shall live."

She gave him such a shining smile that he almost kissed her again. He was halted by the dowager duchess's amused voice. "I'm glad you two found a kissing bough to misbehave under. We wouldn't want the children corrupted."

Anthony and Emma both jumped as if they'd been caught picking pockets. Then they both turned to the dowager, who was gliding over the polished floor toward them.

Calmly she asked, "Did you get Brand and Cecilia sorted out?"

"Yes, Grandmére," Emma replied as if it was perfectly natural for the dowager to know everything. Perhaps it was.

Anthony added, "I suggest that you avoid the gallery. I think they may be reconciling in a manner that would embarrass anyone who accidentally interrupted them."

Amusement gleamed in her blue eyes. "Well done, both of you. Christmas should be a time of reconciliation. By that measure, this may be the best Christmas we've ever had at Harley."

Almost simultaneously, Anthony and Emma said, "It's the best I've ever had!" Then they looked at each, laughing with the sheer pleasure of being in love.

The dowager studied them both thoughtfully. "I've talked to Amelia and James, and they agree that it would be a very good thing for the two of you to exchange your vows again tomorrow night before the Christmas Eve service. That way, the whole family can celebrate with you. Emma, James would like to give you away, if you agree."

Emma inhaled with delight. "I would like that above all things. Anthony?"

"An excellent idea." He put his arm around her waist. "I wonder if Brand would stand up with me? When I was younger, I'd always assumed that some day he would be my best man. This would be a way to put the past behind us."

"I expect that he would be very honored by such a request." Smiling with satisfaction, the dowager turned and floated away.

Emma glanced shyly at Anthony. "I used to dream of being married at Harley. In my wildest dreams, I even imagined marrying you."

"I think a second ceremony will be most appropriate." Anthony drew her into his arms again. "After all, when we married in London, it was a marriage of convenience. This time, my dearest, it will be a pledge of love."

Tears filled Emma's eyes. Wiping at them with one hand, she said tremulously, "Now you're going to think that I'm a watering pot, too."

"As long as you're *my* watering pot," he said tenderly.

Emma laughed and slid her arms around his neck. "If I'm your watering pot, then you're the cleverest bargain I ever made." Her smile turned wicked. "The very best husband money could buy!"

MAD, BAD, AND DANGEROUS
TO KNOW

CHAPTER 1

The Texas Panhandle, 1870s

HE WAS GOING to be hanged on Tuesday.

Andrew Kane supposed that he should be contemplating his imminent demise, but the misery of the present left no room to worry about next week. The bleak, windy plains of the Texas panhandle were dismal at the best of times, and in his present situation, they were a fair approximation of hell.

The horse ahead of him kicked up a swirl of dust and Kane began to cough with parched painfulness. If he didn't get water soon, he wouldn't live long enough to be hanged.

No point in asking his escorts for a drink, though. When Kane had done that yesterday, Biff, the more vicious of the two, had knocked him to the ground, sneering that he wasn't gonna pamper no low-down, murdering son of a bitch.

While Biff underlined his remark with a kick in the ribs, the other temporary deputy, Whittles, had chimed in. "Witless," as Kane mentally dubbed him, had waved a tin cup of water and said that mebbe they'd give the prisoner some if he got down on his knees and asked for it real purty.

Kane might have complied if he thought it would do any good, but he knew his guards were just looking for entertainment. After a good belly laugh over his groveling, Witless would have poured the water on the ground just out of reach.

Tiredly Kane raised his handcuffed wrists and wiped his sweaty forehead with one sleeve. In a couple of hours they would be in Forlorn Hope, the last night's stop before reaching their destination, Prairie City. He supposed that in the interests of keeping him alive for his execution, the sheriff in Prairie City would give him water. It wouldn't do to deprive the crowd that would turn out to see justice visited on the ungodly.

Kane had been to a hanging once, when he had been such a young fool that he'd thought it would be entertaining. The convict had been a skinny little fellow, too light to break his neck when the trap fell away under his feet. The poor devil had swung back and forth for quite a spell, gasping and kicking.

Kane hadn't seen the end; he'd been behind the livery stable, spewing his guts out. He never went to a hanging again. He was no saint, but he sure as hell hadn't expected to end on the gallows himself.

He ran a dry tongue over his cracked lips. As a boy he'd wanted an exciting life, and he'd gotten it. Maybe he should have wished for a little less excitement.

Elizabeth Holden wearily contemplated the yellow dust that saturated her mourning gown. Black wasn't a very practical color in a dusty late Texas autumn, but with both her husband and her father dead in the last month, she didn't have much choice about what to wear. Heaven knew that black suited her mood. She shifted in her saddle, hoping to find a more comfortable position.

A soft southern voice said, "You feeling poorly, Miz Holden?"

Liza managed a smile for her escort. Since there wasn't anything he could do for what ailed her, there was no point in making him worry. "I'm fine, Mr. Jackson, just a little tired. I'll be glad to reach Forlorn Hope. As I recall, the hotel there is a good one."

Tom Jackson nodded, but his dark eyes were still concerned. "Mebbe I can hire a wagon to take you the rest of the way. Mr. Holden will have my hide if anything happens to you."

Liza felt a chill, as if clutching hands were closing around her. Determinedly she shook off the image, not wanting to think of the dreary future that stretched before her. "Truly, I'm fine. The road is so bad that horseback is easier than a wagon would be."

Mr. Jackson nodded, accepting her decision, but the compassion in his eyes almost reduced her to tears. He'd worked for the Holdens for years and must have a fair idea what her life had been like as bride of the late Billie Holden. Not that he could know the worst. Even Billie's parents hadn't known just how difficult their son had been. They hadn't wanted to know.

The rest of the ride was accomplished in silence. The town of Forlorn Hope was better than its name, but not much. Besides the hotel, there were two saloons, a handful of stores, and a couple dozen straggling houses.

The town was on the route between Liza's girlhood home in Willow Point and her in-laws' ranch outside Prairie City, but with her father dead and his general store sold, she'd probably never come this way again. No great loss, she thought dully as her companion helped her from her horse.

After he carried her luggage into the hotel and located a clerk to register her, Liza said, "Didn't you mention that a cousin of yours lived here, Mr. Jackson?"

"Yes, ma'am, the blacksmith." He smiled reminiscently. "His wife Molly is the best Alabama cook in Texas."

"Then take the rest of the day off and go see them," Liza suggested. "Spend the night if you like. We came through in such a hurry two weeks ago that you didn't have time for a visit, so you should make up for that now."

Mr. Jackson hesitated, clearly tempted. "I should stay in the hotel bunkhouse so's I'm nearby if you need anything."

"I won't need anything. I'll take a bath, have some food sent up, and go to bed early," she assured him. "Think of the time off as a thank you for all the help you were with my father's funeral and all."

He surveyed her face, then nodded. "If you're sure, Miz Holden. I'll come for you at nine in the morning."

THE HOT BATH was wonderful for Liza's sore muscles. After she'd soaped and soaked, she lay back in the tin tub and studied her body, trying to see if her abdomen was starting to enlarge. But she could detect no change. If anything, she'd lost weight in the last weeks. Hard to imagine that a baby was growing inside her.

Not a baby. Her jailer.

Desolation swept through her, but before tears could destroy her fragile composure, she climbed from the tub and briskly toweled herself dry. She must not allow herself to sink into melancholy, for she needed all her strength.

Thinking that she'd read a bit before going to bed, Liza donned her other black dress, which was wrinkled but clean. Then she began brushing out her wheat-blond hair. It was still light outside, so she drifted to the window and gazed idly down into the street. A half dozen people were in sight, none of them in any great hurry.

Her eye was caught by the wreckage of a recently burned building. Thinking back, she recalled that there had been a combined town office and jail on the site before.

She was about to turn away from the window when three dusty riders appeared. Curiously she saw that one of the horses was on a lead, and the black-clad rider on its back was slumped forward as if barely able to stay upright.

When the newcomers were opposite the hotel, the heavyset man in the lead saw the charred ruins of the jail. Scowling ferociously, he halted the group right under Liza's window, so close that she could see his small, piggy eyes.

After asking a question of a loafer sitting in front of the hotel, Pig-Eyes dismounted and tethered his horse to the hitching rail. Then he went to the led horse, whose rider wore the characteristic black suit, ruffled shirt, and brocade waistcoat of a gambler.

Pig-Eyes grabbed the gambler's arm and jerked him from his saddle. The man in black pitched heavily from his mount, barely managing to catch his saddle horn in time to prevent himself from crashing to the ground.

As he regained his balance, Liza saw that his hands were cuffed together. A prisoner. She wondered what he'd done.

The third rider, a thin, weasely fellow, dismounted and laid a rough hand on the gambler's arm. In spite of his physical condition, there was defiance in the prisoner's posture as he raised his head and answered back.

The results were explosive. With a snarl of fury, Weasel drew back his fist and slugged the other man in the stomach.

As the gambler folded over, he kicked viciously at his tormentor, his boot connecting just below the knee. Weasel howled and almost collapsed. When he recovered, he and Pig-Eyes began beating and kicking the prisoner. Even when he fell to the ground, the kicks and blows continued, right under Liza's horrified gaze.

Fury blazed through her, burning away her fatigue and depression. Without waiting to see more, she raced from her room, taking the stairs two at a time, her loose hair flying behind her.

When she reached the street, she saw that a half dozen townspeople were watching the beating. Though most looked uncomfortable, no one intervened. It wasn't healthy to come between angry, armed men and their victim.

Liza was too incensed to feel such compunction. She cried, "Stop that this instant, you brutes!"

From sheer surprise, Pig-Eyes and Weasel obeyed, both turning to stare at her. Liza took advantage of the pause to say fiercely, "You should be ashamed of yourselves, beating a man who is bound and helpless!"

Weasel shifted uncomfortably, his bravado vanishing in the presence of a lady. "Beggin' your pardon, ma'am, but Andrew Kane ain't helpless. He's quicker'n a snake and twice as mean."

"That doesn't give you the right to beat him to

death," Liza retorted. "What kind of men are you, to attack someone who can't defend himself?"

She looked down at the gambler, who lay still in the dusty street, blood flowing from numerous cuts. Under the dirt and bruises he looked young and vulnerable, not mean at all. Not that Liza was much of a judge of character. When she met Billie Holden, she'd thought he was kind and honorable.

A lean man with drooping mustaches and a tin badge on his vest pushed through the small crowd of silent onlookers. "I'm Sheriff Taylor," he barked. "What's going on here?"

Pig-Eyes said, "My name's Biff Burns. Me and my partner Whittles are temporary deputies who are taking this murderer to Prairie City for hangin'."

He prodded his prisoner with one booted toe. "We was gonna put him in the jail for the night, but I see it's burnt down."

The sheriff scowled. "It was fired by some folks from Rapid City. They want to see their town made county seat, so they burned down our public building."

Uninterested in local politics, Burns said, "Where can we put this son of a bitch tonight?" The weasel hissed something and Burns flushed and glanced at Liza. "Beggin' your pardon, ma'am."

After giving him an icy glance, she knelt by Kane. Burns exclaimed, "Don't get so close, ma'am! He's dangerous."

Ignoring the words, Liza took her handkerchief and began blotting blood from a slash on the man's forehead.

Long, dark lashes flickered open to reveal eyes of piercing blue. Gambler's eyes that saw everything and gave away nothing.

For a long moment their gazes held. She saw intelligence, shrewdness, anger, and determination in the blue depths. The qualities of a man used to living on the edge of danger. It was suddenly easy to believe that he was a murderer. Disconcerted, Liza sat back on her heels.

Yet when he spoke, Kane was polite enough. "A pleasure to make your acquaintance, darlin'." He had a crisp accent that she couldn't identify because his voice was a barely audible rasp.

Seeing his cracked lips, Liza asked, "Do you need water?"

Desperate longing flared in his eyes, though he tried to keep his voice steady. "I'd be much obliged, ma'am."

She glanced up at Burns. "Please give me your canteen."

Biff started to protest, then subsided, unwilling to argue with a lady in front of a steadily growing audience. He untied the canteen and handed it to Liza.

She twisted out the stopper and carefully dribbled a few drops into Kane's mouth. His tanned throat moved convulsively as he swallowed. Slowly she poured more, careful not to give him more than he could manage.

From the way he drank, she guessed that it had been a long time since he'd been given water. Her anger rose again. He might be a murderer, but even a mad dog didn't deserve such treatment.

The sheriff said, "You can put your prisoner in the

hotel storeroom, Burns. It's got a solid door that locks and a window too small for a man to get through. Won't be the first time it held a prisoner. He'll be safe there for the night."

Burns nodded thanks. "We'll lock 'im up as soon as the lady gets out of the way."

Liza glanced up, her gaze going to the sheriff, who seemed reasonable. "This man needs medical attention."

Sheriff Taylor shook his head. "There's no doctor in Forlorn Hope."

Liza got to her feet and gave Burns a challenging glance. "Then I'll tend him myself."

Outraged, Biff said, "Nothin' wrong with that son of a..." Remembering his language, he coughed. "He's not bad hurt, ma'am, and 'sides, in a coupla days it won't matter. A lady shouldn't concern herself with trash like him."

Liza's eyes narrowed. "Sheriff Taylor, the American constitution forbids cruel and unusual punishment. Doesn't that mean that even prisoners deserve food, water, and medical treatment?"

The sheriff shrugged. "If the lady wants to play nursemaid, let her. Most gamblers have a soft spot for women, so he probably won't hurt her, though you might want to chain him up, just in case."

Burns and Whittles grabbed Kane by the upper arms and hauled him to his feet. Not wanting to watch, Liza stalked back into the hotel.

She didn't understand her need to champion a criminal who probably deserved everything he got, but the impulse was too strong to deny. Perhaps it was because she felt so helpless about her own life. By taking shameless advantage of the reverence westerners had for women, she could do something to help a fellow being.

It was a nice bonus that her good deed would also keep her too busy to think about her own problems, at least for a while.

LIZA SPENT the next half hour collecting what she would need to treat Kane's wounds, plus food and drink since the deputies couldn't be trusted to feed their prisoner. She also took a folded blanket since in December, it got cold at night.

It was almost dark by the time she made her way to the storeroom, which lay behind a larger chamber which was used as a second dining room when the hotel was busy. The only occupant was Biff. His chair was tilted back and his booted feet rested on the edge of a table while he idly shuffled cards and looked bored.

When Liza entered, the deputy's expression brightened and the front legs of the chair hit the floor with a bang. The frank admiration in his gaze made her grateful for the fact that she was wearing mourning. Even the Biffs of the world would seldom force unwelcome flirtation on a new widow.

She nodded toward an unused lantern sitting on the

sideboard. "Will you light that and bring it in, Mr. Burns?" As he hastened to comply, she murmured, "You're very kind."

The deputy opened the door to the storeroom and she stepped inside. It made a good cell, for the only window was high on the wall and too small to be used by anyone but a child. The walls were lined with shelves, and sacks, barrels, and boxes were stacked around the walls. The prisoner had been dumped unceremoniously in the middle of the plank floor.

Though Kane had been lying motionless, his eyes flickered open when they entered. Accompanied by a metallic rattle, he pushed his battered body up so that he was sitting against a sack of flour. Liza saw that his left handcuff had been removed from his wrist, then locked to a chain that looped around a supporting post in the corner. Though he had one hand free and the chain was long enough to allow some movement, she disliked seeing a man treated like a dog on a leash.

Wanting to get rid of the deputy and his hungry stare, she said, "You've had a long, hard ride, Mr. Burns." She set her tray on the floor near Kane. "There's no need for you to stay here if you'd rather go to the saloon for a bite of supper."

Biff licked his lips as duty wrestled with desire. "I shouldn't leave you alone with him, ma'am."

"Your prisoner is in no condition to hurt anyone," she said mildly. "If he does get rambunctious, I'll just move out of reach."

"I'll have to lock you in," Biff warned. "Can't risk letting him break out."

She shrugged. "As you wish. It's going to take time to clean his wounds. You can let me out when you've finished your own dinner."

"That's what I'll do, then," Biff decided. He hung the lantern from a nail so its soft rays illuminated most of the storeroom, then turned and left.

Kane had been watching in silence, but as the key turned in the door, locking them in together, he drawled, "He's right, darlin'. You shouldn't be here. Twelve good men and true have decided that I am mad, bad, and dangerous to know."

Her eyes widened, and not only because of his cool English accent. Who would have thought a murderer would be so well-educated? Well, she had had a decent education, too, reading every book that had come through her father's store. "Don't try to convince me that you're Lord Byron," she said briskly, "because I am certainly not Lady Caroline Lamb."

Startled pleasure lit Kane's tanned face and his tension eased. "If you're not Lady Caroline Lamb, who are you?" He examined her with appreciative interest. "Guardian angels aren't supposed to be so luscious-looking."

She found herself coloring under his scrutiny. Not wanting to use the married name that she had come to hate, she replied, "My name is Liza. You're an Englishman?"

"I was born in England, but I'm an American now. I came here when I was twenty-one."

"Are you a remittance man?"

"My family didn't actually pay me to keep out of sight," he said with a crooked smile, "but they did heave a vast sigh of relief when I decided to see the world after I was sent down from Oxford. That means I was thrown out," he added when he saw that she didn't understand the term. "The professors said that I lacked a proper respect for rules and tradition. They were right."

"Many of your countrymen must feel the same way, because there are plenty of them rambling around this part of the world." She'd always enjoyed the Britons who stopped by her father's store, and had encouraged them to talk just so she could listen to their lovely accents. Kane himself spoke with a delicious blend of English crispness and American idiom.

After dipping a pad of cotton into the bowl of warm water, she began cleaning the lacerations on Kane's face. Under the cuts, dust, and several days' growth of beard, she discovered that his features were strong boned and handsome. She guessed that he'd broken his share of female hearts. His intense blue eyes were disturbing at such close range.

He winced when she touched the deepest gash, which started on his forehead and curved down his left temple. Thinking that conversation would distract him from the discomfort, she asked, "What made you decide to stay in this country?"

"When I first reached Denver, I went to a livery stable to rent a horse. The only man in sight was a rough-looking chap sitting on a stump, so I asked him where his master was. He spat a stream of tobacco juice that just missed my foot, then said that the son of a bitch hadn't been born yet." Kane chuckled. "I knew instantly I'd found my spiritual home. Excuse the profanity, but cleaning up the fellow's language would dilute the flavor of the encounter."

Liza smiled, unoffended. She was tolerant of ungenteel language, for her father's customers were frequently profane. She had found it touching when tall, bristly cowhands blushed and apologized with the shyness of little boys. But Kane was another sort of man entirely, one who was completely sure of himself even now, when he was on the verge of execution.

The thought produced a jolt of disorientation. It was impossible, obscene, that the man beneath her hands would soon be dead. He was too alive, too vividly real. Distressed, she bowed her head and moistened a pad with whiskey, then patted the cuts she had already cleaned.

Though the alcohol must have stung like blazes, he endured it stoically. When she had finished working on his face, he remarked, "A pity to waste good whiskey on cleaning wounds when I'm going to die anyway."

She chuckled and reached for the china mug. "I should have guessed you might want a drink more than nursing."

"A sign of weakness on my part," he said with self-mockery, "but the last fortnight has been ... difficult. I wouldn't mind a bit of oblivion."

"I don't think there's enough here for oblivion," she said as she poured whiskey from the small bottle. "Will you settle for relaxation?"

Kane laughed out loud. Strange. He hadn't expected to laugh again before he died. Nor had he expected to be alone with a beautiful young lady. He feasted his eyes on her, for she was the loveliest sight he had seen in years. The loveliest he was likely to see for the rest of his life.

To his regret, she had pinned up the thick fair hair that had danced loose around her shoulders when she had come charging out of the hotel, but a few wheat-colored tendrils still curled temptingly around her face.

And what a face it was! Heart-shaped, with delicate features and wondrous gray eyes that regarded the world without flinching. The women were one of the things he liked most about America. The best of them were direct, confident, as strong as a man, not at all like the simpering misses he'd known in England.

After putting the mug into his left hand, Liza turned her attention to his right wrist, the one that was still shackled. Her lips pursed when she pushed the cuff up and discovered that the metal had gouged a circle of ugly lacerations. Without comment, she began cleaning the raw flesh. Her light, cool fingers were soothing as she washed and bandaged his right wrist, then the equally damaged left one.

He sipped the whiskey slowly, wanting it to last. It hit hard on an empty stomach. He welcomed the harsh burn, for it eased the aches and pains he'd suffered at the hands of the deputies. The whiskey affected him in other ways, too, and when Liza bent forward, he had to fight an impulse to pull out her hair pins.

Yet much as he would have enjoyed releasing the sun streaked brilliance of her hair, he restrained himself. He daren't alarm her, for he needed her kindness too much. Already he hated the knowledge that soon she would leave.

Indicating the widow's weeds with his forefinger, he said, "You've had a loss?"

She went still. "Two," she said quietly. "Several weeks ago, my husband was killed. Right after we buried him, I received word that my father had also died. I'm returning to my in-laws' ranch from my father's funeral."

"I'm so sorry," he said, knowing how inadequate the words were. Needing to know she'd be all right, he continued, "Your husband's family will look out for you?"

"Oh, yes," she said with a trace of bitterness. "Since I have something they want, I'll be very well cared for."

When her hand unconsciously went to her belly, he realized that she must be with child. It was a surprise and not only because of her slimness, for she didn't have the glow common to expectant mothers. He supposed that the tragedies she had experienced were enough to extinguish joy. "At least you'll have something left of your husband," he said, wanting to offer comfort.

Her face tightened and she almost spoke. Then she gave a faint shake of her head and glanced up. "Are you hungry, Mr. Kane? I brought some food."

Her face was only a foot from his, close enough so that he could admire the creamy texture of her skin and the alluring fullness of her mouth. A wave of desire swept through him, so intense that he had to bite his lip to prevent himself from reacting. In a detached corner of his mind, he knew that what he felt was not simply normal male yearning for a lovely woman, but a desperate desire to bury himself in passion; to obliterate, for a moment, the terror of knowing how little time he had left.

Exercising all of his will, he said steadily, "It's been so long since I ate that I've forgotten what food is, so I reckon that it's time I had some. And if I'm to call you Liza, you must call me Drew." His smile was a little crooked. "Normal manners don't quite seem to fit present circumstances."

"Very well, Drew." Her tray included slices of cold fried chicken and slabs of fresh bread, which made a tasty sandwich. As he ate, he felt strength flowing into his exhausted muscles. He hadn't realized how much hunger was affecting him.

When he finished, Liza said, "Would you like more?"

He shook his head. "That's all I can manage at the moment, but I thank you kindly. Amazing what food can do for one's state of mind. I feel better than I have in days."

As she covered the rest of the food, a gunshot punctuated the night air. Kane frowned as he realized that the noise outside had been steadily increasing. "From the racket, it sounds like every cowhand in fifty miles has come to town to celebrate payday."

Liza jumped when an exuberant bellow sounded right under their window. "I hope Sheriff Taylor can handle them!"

"He seemed like a capable man." Kane cocked his head, trying to decipher the conflicting voices. "My guess is that hands from two or three rival spreads are entertaining themselves by trying to rip each other's heads off."

She shivered and glanced at the door. "They wouldn't break into the hotel looking for food or whiskey, would they?"

"Even if they do, we'll be safe here. Besides the key lock, there's a bar for the door. Whoever built this hotel was a cautious soul." He got to his feet and went for the wooden bar leaning in a shadowed corner, only to be pulled up with a painful jerk when he reached the end of the chain.

He swore under his breath. In the pleasure of Liza's company, he had forgotten his restraints. "I'm afraid that if you want the extra protection, you'll have to do it yourself."

She retrieved the heavy bar and dropped it in place with a solid *thunk*. "This will stop any drunken cowboys who might want to get too friendly."

A burst of shots sounded from the direction of the saloon, followed by the tinkle of breaking glass. The sheriff would have his work cut out for him. Kane frowned. "Since Biff and Witless are acting deputies,

Sheriff Taylor will probably enlist them to help him whip that lot into line. Might be hours before you get let out. Sorry."

"No need to apologize." She gracefully seated herself on a sack of flour. "It's not your fault."

"Maybe I'm apologizing because I'm not sorry you're marooned here," he said in a burst of candor. After days of having to maintain a stiff upper lip while surrounded by enemies, the need to have one last real, human conversation was overpowering. "Thanks for helping a dangerous, unworthy stranger, Liza. It... means a great deal to me."

She tucked her feet under her, carefully covering her ankles with her skirt. "You don't seem very dangerous. And I'm not being entirely unselfish. It's ... been hard making it through the nights. Distraction is welcome." Then, speaking quickly, as if she had said too much, she continued with deliberate lightness, "Are you a gambler, or do you just dress like one?"

Kane was still standing, for now that he was stronger he felt restless. Accompanied by a soft clinking of chain, he began to pace back and forth within the limits of his tether. "I was a gambler for years, but I'd given that up."

"Why did you do that?"

"I wanted something different. Better." He stopped in front of the small window and gazed out, seeing not the clear night sky but the long, winding road that had led him to this impromptu cell. "I come from a long line of English squires, respectable folk who wanted nothing more than to work their land, raise another generation of little Kanes, and be buried in English soil. If I'd been in line to inherit the estate, I expect I would have been exactly like all my ancestors. But by custom the land goes to the oldest son, and I was the younger."

He turned and leaned against the wall, his arms folded across his chest. "I couldn't have the estate and didn't have the patience for the church, the army, or the law, which are the usual choices for younger sons. So I became a hellion instead. After being sent down from Oxford, I came to America, which suited me right down to the ground. For years, I lived in saloons, moved from one town to the next when I got bored, saw the world and lived high. I gambled with some of the best, and won more often than not."

"Did you win honestly?" she asked, curious rather than condemning.

He smiled a little. "I always played straight in an honest game, but if I sat down with a bunch of crooks, I could cheat as well as any riverboat gambler. It was a point of pride." His smile faded and deep weariness showed. "But after seven or eight years, I'd had enough. Too much time in dark, smoky, noisy saloons, living on bad coffee and hard liquor. Too many sore losers who'll pull a gun rather than admit they'd played their cards badly. It got downright tedious."

He looked down at his hands and fiddled absently with the metal cuff. "It's ironic. I was the family rebel and black sheep. I traveled thousands of miles to the wild frontier, braving Red Indians and prairie buffalo and Lord knows what else. My mother says that my letters are a source of shocked fascination to the whole county of Wiltshire. But when my thirtieth birthday showed on the horizon, I learned that at heart, I'm exactly like all my respectable ancestors. What I really wanted was a piece of land to call my own." He fell silent.

Liza waited patiently for him to continue. When he didn't, she asked, "Have you been looking for a spread to buy?"

"I already found one. Bought it with the proceeds of a four-day poker game in Leadville." He smiled wistfully. "It's up in Colorado, in the foothills above Pueblo. A valley with plenty of water, mountains all around. The most beautiful place I've ever seen. And only a couple of hours from a railroad. I can be in Denver in less than a day when I feel a need for civilization."

He sighed. "At least, I could have if I wanted to. I only lived at the Lazy K for six months. Not long enough to get bored. I made friends with the ranch hands and neighbors, gave money to the church fund, and even let myself be adopted by a dog named Jenny."

"There's nothing like a dog to make a house feel like home," Liza commented.

"The Lazy K felt like home from the day I moved in. I'd been looking forward to having a real English Christmas like when I was a child in Wiltshire. A decorated tree in the parlor and candles in all the windows from Christmas Eve until Epiphany." His eyes were distant with memory. "Candles to welcome travelers, my mother always said. She always gave a grand holiday dinner for family and neighbors. Still does, actually."

"It sounds like you had lovely holiday celebrations," Liza said warmly.

His expression shuttered and he gave an indifferent shrug. "Long ago and far way. I was a damned fool to think of doing anything like that at the Lazy K."

"It's not foolish to create a home." Liza regarded him with wide, compassionate eyes. "You don't look like a murderer to me. Were you falsely convicted?"

He laughed bitterly. "Oh, I killed a man right enough. Everyone in the Gilded Rooster that night agreed that it was self-defense, but the fellow I shot was a rich man's son, so justice didn't have a chance."

Her eyes widened and the blood drained from her face until she was pale as a death mask. "What was the name of the man you killed?"

"Holden. Billie Holden." He frowned. "Did you know him?"

Looking ill, she buried her face in shaking hands. "He was my husband," she said dully.

CHAPTER 3

DEAR GOD, this lovely girl couldn't have been that brute's wife! Kane thought with horror. Instinctively, he retreated as far from her as the chain would allow. He would have given everything he had ever possessed to be somewhere else, any place on earth where he wouldn't be causing Billie Holden's widow more pain. "I'm sorry," he said helplessly. "So damned *sorry!*"

She raised her head and regarded him with wide, stark eyes. "How did it happen?"

Hesitantly, he said, "It was quick. Your husband didn't suffer any. Beyond that..." Kane shook his head miserably. "You don't need to know more than that, Mrs. Holden."

"Liza. My name is Liza." She got to her feet and approached him, eyes dry and implacable. "And I do need to know. All his father said was that Billie had been gunned down in a saloon called the Gilded Rooster, but there's more to it than that, isn't there?" When he still hesitated, she said tensely, "I must know, Drew!"

He released his breath with a sigh. "Very well. I'd come down into Texas to look over some fancy new stock I'd heard about, and was on my way home when it happened. I stopped for the night in Saline. After dinner, I sat down for a friendly game of poker at the Gilded Rooster with a couple of locals.

"I was about to call it a night when there was a row at the bar. A chap who'd had too much to drink— Holden— took a fancy to a girl. Not one of the regular sporting girls, who'd have been happy to accommodate him, but a little Chinese kitchen maid who'd brought out a tray of clean glasses. Mei-Lin couldn't have been more than fourteen or fifteen. Holden—"

He broke off. "Are you sure you want to hear this? Only a man who was dead drunk and crazy could even think of looking at another female when he had a wife like you waiting at home."

Grimly she said, "Keep talking!"

Reluctantly Kane continued, "Holden wouldn't take no for an answer, and he was scaring Mei-Lin half to death. The other men in the saloon didn't like it, but none of them dared interfere. One of the bar girls, Red Sally, tried to break it up. Even though she looked almost as scared as Mei-Lin, she said she'd be happy to go upstairs with such a fine gent. Holden ignored her. Said he'd never had a Chink, so he was going to have this one. He grabbed Mei-Lin by the wrist and started to drag her away.

"When she began crying, I ambled over and suggested that it might be better to choose a lady of experience. Instead of answering, Holden hauled off and slugged me in the stomach. I went down hard, and the next thing I knew, I was staring at the business end of a Colt.

"As I rolled away, Holden put a bullet into the floor where my head had been. I had a derringer in my pocket, so I shot back before he could try again." Kane fingered the scorched hole in his coat where he had fired through the fabric. "If there had been any warning, I'd have tried to wing him rather than shooting to kill, but it all happened so fast…" His voice trailed off.

"If it was self-defense, how come you were convicted?"

His glance was sardonic. "You probably know that your husband was visiting his uncle, Matt Sloan, who pretty much owns Saline. Sloan decided that his nephew had to be avenged, so he sent a posse of his hands after me the next day. I was easy to catch, since I thought I'd been cleared and wasn't trying to hide. When they caught up, they took me back to Saline, where Sloan called a court in the bar of the Gilded Rooster. The saloon owner, who was a crony of Sloan's, sat as judge."

Kane's mouth twisted. "No witnesses were called, and whenever I tried to talk myself, I was ruled out of order with a fist. I was tried, convicted, and condemned in ten minutes. Sloan sent word of what he'd done to Holden's family.

"Your father-in-law requested that I be sent to Prairie City so the family could have the pleasure of seeing me hang. Biff and Witless are a couple of Sloan's hands who were deputized to take me back. The hanging must have been organized after you left to bury your father. It should be quite an event." His agonized gaze caught hers. "I wish I could change what happened, but I can't. I'm sorry."

She turned away and leaned against the wall, wrapping her arms around herself as if she were freezing. After a long, painful silence, she said, "Don't blame yourself. Billie was a walking calamity. If it hadn't been you, sooner or later someone would have had to kill him." She gave a shuddering sigh. "His parents spoiled him rotten all his life. He was always nice as pie to them, and they thought he could do no wrong."

Knowing it was none of his business, Kane asked, "Why did you marry him?"

She smiled sadly, her mind in the past. "He could be charming, and of course he was handsome as sin. When he came to Willow Point three years ago, he seemed like every girl's dream come true. My father wasn't so sure, but I was so crazy in love that Papa was afraid I'd run off if he didn't let us get married. He'd heard of the Holden family, so he knew that I'd be marrying a man who could support me.

"But things started going wrong as soon as Billie took me back to Prairie City. His parents were furious that he'd married a nobody. They'd had hopes of matching him up with the daughter of another big rancher. But since the deed was done, they had to accept me. They were civil on the surface, but except for his sister Janie, it was like living in an icebox. Worst of all, Billie changed.

Sometimes it was like when we were courting, but more often ..." Her voice trailed off.

"What was he like then?"

Haltingly she said, "About six months after we married ..." She stopped, her face white, before finishing in a rush of words. "At a church social, Billie saw me laughing with a neighbor. He pulled me away, and as soon as we got home he went crazy. Claimed I'd betrayed him, then he beat me to within an inch of my life."

She bent her head, tears glinting in her eyes. "I was laid up for a long time. There was no one I could talk to. When I tried to tell his mother what happened, she wouldn't listen. Billie had said I'd fallen down the stairs, and that was that."

Kane swore with suppressed violence. "Where was your husband when you were half-dead from what he'd done?"

"Billie was very apologetic," she said in a brittle voice. "Got down on his knees and begged my forgiveness, swore he'd never hurt me again."

"Did he keep his word?" Kane asked cynically, knowing the answer.

"He never got quite so crazy again, but whenever he drank, he'd knock me around," she said painfully. "He started taking long trips, supposedly doing business for his father. And ... and he began seeing other women. He didn't try to hide it from me."

If Billie Holden had been present, Kane would have broken the polecat's neck with his bare hands. "Did you consider leaving him?"

"I did, but... well, he was my husband, for better and for worse. Sometimes he wasn't so bad, and I kept thinking that if I tried harder, was a better wife, he wouldn't be the way he was."

"No! Don't blame yourself," Kane said sharply. "Any man who'd treat his wife like he treated you is crazy or evil."

She looked down at her fretfully twisting fingers. "I expect you're right. No matter what I did, it didn't make a difference." Silent tears began flowing down her face. "God help me," she whispered, "when I heard he was dead, my first reaction was relief."

Kane had never been able to stand seeing a lady cry. Without conscious thought, he reached out and stroked her bent head as if she were a hurt child. It wouldn't have surprised him if she had jerked away, but she didn't. Instead, she turned into his arms with a muffled sob.

He held her close while she wept as if her heart was breaking. He wondered when she had last been able to cry. Living in a house where she was despised, with a brutal husband who didn't appreciate the treasure he had married.... God, it was enough to convince a man there was no justice in the world.

When her sobs began to diminish, he said quietly, "In time the nightmare will be over, Liza. When you leave the Holden ranch, you'll be able to build a new life. You'll find the love and happiness you deserve."

She made a choked, hysterical sound. "It will never be over." Her hand went to her abdomen. "I'm pregnant.

His parents will never let me go because they want Billie's child. I'll be trapped in that house until I die."

Kane was silent for a long time. Then he sat down against the wall, bringing her with him and arranging her across his lap so that her head was resting against his shoulder. She was soft, so soft.

"It's a bad situation, Liza, but not hopeless," he said as he circled his arms around her. "You don't have to go back to the Holdens. There's plenty of ways a hard-working woman can support herself. When you're ready to marry again, there will be no shortage of decent men who will treat you right."

"I've thought of all the possibilities," she said bleakly. "I've thought of nothing else. If I didn't go back, or tried to leave with the baby, they'd hunt me down no matter where I went. I'd never have a moment free of worrying when they'd find us. And with his money, sooner or later Mr. Holden *would* find us. He'd never stop until he did."

Kane's arms tightened around her. "You don't have to stay after your confinement. Though it would be a hard, hard thing to do, you could leave and let the baby be raised by its grandparents. Or would they insist that you stay, too?"

"The Holdens wouldn't mind if I left after the baby is born. I'm sure they'd be delighted to see the last of me. But how can I let them raise my child? Billie was probably born with a mean streak, but they made him worse." She swallowed hard. "Though it's a terrible thing to admit, I don't even want this baby. I've had a feeling of doom ever since I found out. What if the child turns out like Billie? Even if I'm there, I might not be able to make a difference. Yet I can't abandon my own child. I *can't!*"

"Life is harder for good people," he said sadly, unsurprised at her answer.

Liza closed her eyes, her grief ebbing away. Shouting and occasional gunshots rattled in the distance. She hoped the trouble would last all night, because when the town quieted down, Biff Burns would surely return and she would have to leave. Strange that in the arms of her husband's killer, she was finding peace. Strange, yet it felt utterly right. She couldn't blame Andrew Kane for what had happened in the Gilded Rooster. He was a decent man who'd tried to help a terrified young girl, and he was going to pay for his decency with his life.

Thinking about it, she realized that she and Drew were both victims of Billie's craziness. Maybe that was why she felt so much kinship with him.

No, it was more than that. Drew was special. She would have thought so under any circumstances. "Thank you for listening," she murmured. "My problems aren't much compared to yours. Your courage sets a good example for me."

There was a harsh edge to his laughter. "You think I have courage? Believe me, it's as fake as a wooden nickel. Though I've faced death before, it's always been a sudden thing, with no time to think. That's not so hard, but having to sit and wait to die ..." He inhaled, then said in a rush of words, "I'm scared, Liza. Not only of death, but of having to die in front of a crowd of strangers. I'm terrified that when they take me to the gallows, I'll break down and bawl like a wounded steer, begging for my life like the yellow-bellied coward I am." His voice broke.

When he spoke again, it was with hard self-mockery. "Pretty stupid to worry about whether I'm going to die with a proper British stiff upper lip. But with death the only thing left to me, how I do it seems powerfully important."

She raised her head and studied Drew's face. In the dim golden lamplight, the planes of his face seemed unyielding as granite. She guessed that when the time came, he would not disgrace his solid Wiltshire ancestors. He would face death with composure, perhaps even a dry joke. Yet she understood his fear. Merciful heaven, how she understood it!

On impulse, she leaned forward and touched her lips to his, wanting to convey her sympathy, her gratitude, her belief in his courage. After a startled moment, his arms tightened around her waist and he kissed her back, crushing her against the hard angles of his body.

Liza was not surprised by the sweetness, but she was shaken by the fire that flared between them. Even when she was an adoring bride, she had not felt like this. Her mouth opened under his and her head tilted back as she lost herself in the depths of his kiss.

The kiss ended when he lifted his head, saying hoarsely, "It's ... it's time to stop, darlin'."

She opened her eyes, disoriented by the hammering of her own heart. Or perhaps it was his heart she felt, beating in tandem with hers.

"I don't want to stop," she whispered, knowing that

what she was suggesting should have been outrageous. Unthinkable.

Would have been, before tonight, but the last hour had stripped them both down to raw emotion. She knew that he wanted her, for desire was blazoned across his face. If her body would give him solace, she would give it freely.

More than that, she wanted the closeness of being lovers; she wanted a man's touch to obliterate the failure and pain she had too often experienced in her marriage bed. And, ironically, her unwanted pregnancy meant that she could give herself to Drew without fear of consequences.

"Are you sure?" he asked, a hard pulse beating in his jaw. "You've been hurt too much, Liza. I don't want to add to that."

"You won't." She managed a shaky smile. "I'm afraid of what lies ahead, Drew, but maybe I'll be able to face it better if I have something happy to remember." She raised her hands and slipped her fingers into his hair. "Let's forget the world outside this room for as long as we can."

CHAPTER 4

AFTER LIZA SPOKE, Drew wordlessly raised his left hand and began tugging the pins from her hair. One by one, the heavy coils fell around her shoulders. "You are so beautiful." He buried his hands in the tangled, silken mass. "As beautiful as life itself." Leaning forward, he pressed his lips to her throat through the shimmering strands.

She inhaled sharply, startled at the sensations that flared through her as Drew's firm, knowing lips drifted up to her ear, then back to her eager mouth. Slowly, as if they had all the time in the world, he flipped the blanket she'd brought out on the floor. They he laid her back on the blanket, improvising a pillow from two empty burlap sacks.

As he lay down beside her, the chain on his wrist rattled against the planks in an unbearably poignant reminder of what the future held. With sudden desperation she drew him into her arms, tugging up his shirttails so she could touch the warm bare skin of his back. The only thing that mattered was now, this precious, fleeting moment.

The world would judge her wicked, yet she could not believe that what they were doing was wrong. Yes, Kane was a stranger, the man who had killed her husband, but their pain made them kin, and the tenderness between them was balm to her bruised soul.

What followed astonished her. Three years she had been married, and she had thought that she knew all about what a man might do to a woman.

But now, as Drew worshiped her with hands and mouth, she discovered what it was to make love. He kissed every sensitive bit of exposed skin—her throat, her palms, the fragile flesh inside her wrists. And as he did, he whispered how lovely she was, how much joy she was giving him.

She wished that they shared the soft privacy of a bed, with loose garments that might be pushed aside so that flesh could press flesh. That wasn't possible, not when Biff might return and start pounding on the door at any moment. Yet even through the sober layers of her clothing, her breasts came to yearning life when he caressed them.

She tensed when he unbuttoned her drawers and tugged them off. In the past, intimacy had often meant pain, and the taut hunger on his face frightened her a little. But to her surprise he did not immediately mount her. Instead, he pleasured her with slow, expert fingers that created embarrassing amounts of heat and moisture.

Only when her hips began to move involuntarily did he unfasten his trousers and lift himself over her.

They came together easily. Not only was there no hint of pain, but she found that his weight and warmth brought the most profound sense of completion she had ever known. Delighted, she experimentally moved against him.

Her action was like a spark to tinder. He groaned and thrust deeper and suddenly they were mating fiercely, becoming one with sweet, desperate savagery. Her nails curved into the hard, flexing muscles of his back. There were no words, for none were needed. Until, at the end, her body spun out of her control and she cried out with wonder and joy.

As she did, he groaned and drove into her again and again, with a primal rhythm that shattered them both. When he had nothing left to give, he eased forward, surrounding her with his warmth, resting his face in her hair.

When she could speak, she said with awe, "I didn't know it could be like that for a woman."

"You've never... ?"

She shook her head, feeling ridiculously shy. "Never."

Selfishly, he was glad. Though he wished her a happy future with all his heart, he hoped she wouldn't forget the man with whom she had discovered a woman's passion.

He rolled over and sat back across the sack of flour, then lifted her so that she lay across him, one bare leg between his, her skirts rippling about them. "Thank you,

Liza, for a gift beyond price," he said softly as he pulled the blanket over her against the night chill. "You've put the heart back in me. Whatever happens in the next few days, I think I'll be able to face it like a man."

Her fingers curled into the ruffles at the throat of his shirt. "I feel the same way. No matter how bad things get in the future, I'll always have tonight to remember," she said tightly. "If only ..." She stopped, unable to continue.

"Don't say it, sweetheart," he murmured as he stroked her nape with gentle fingers. "Don't even think it. Be glad we're together now. There will be time enough for grief later."

He still didn't quite believe the miracle in his arms. Liza was a lifetime of joy compressed into a handful of minutes. She, who had so little reason to trust, had given herself with brave honesty, and the poignancy of their union was like an arrow in his heart. He wished that he could stop time, with her forever in his embrace.

But that wasn't possible. The din from the riotous cowboys was fading. How much longer would they have? He offered a fervent mental prayer that Biff would do some drinking in the saloon before remembering that he must release the lady from the condemned man's cell.

Knowledge that time was running out was like a clock ticking in the back of his brain. Reluctantly he said, "Better put your hair up, Liza. Anyone seeing you would have a pretty fair idea of what you've been up to."

Blushing, she sat up and began combing her fingers through her hair in a doomed attempt to straighten it. "I must look like a saloon girl."

Enjoying her less-than-successful efforts to look prim, he said appreciatively, "Not at all. You look like a woman who has been well loved."

Her blush deepened, but she didn't avert her eyes.

When she began pinning her hair back, he said, "Liza, I've a favor to ask."

"Anything," she said simply.

"It's a pretty big favor. Someone will have to notify my family of my death. I should write myself, but I can't. Saying, 'By the time you get this, I'll be dead...' Well, I've tried again and again in my head, and I can't get it right. Cowardice again."

After a long pause, he said painfully, "When I bought the Lazy K, I thought that in a year or so, when the place was fixed up the way I wanted, I'd invite my parents for a visit. Maybe even for Christmas. I wanted them to see that the prodigal son hadn't gone as thoroughly to hell as they had feared. But it looks like their fears weren't misplaced."

"Where should I send the letter?" she asked, wanting to lift the darkness that had settled on his face.

"Sir Geoffrey Kane and Lady Kane, Westlands, Amesbury, Wiltshire, England," he replied.

After repeating it twice, she said, "Your father's a lord?"

"No, just a baronet. Sort of a jumped-up ranch owner, English-style."

She smiled at the irreverent description. "Do you want me to tell them the truth?"

"No!" he said harshly. "Tell them that a horse threw

me, or that a fever carried me off! Anything but that I was hanged for murder. No point in their suffering more than necessary."

"Do you have any special messages?"

The muscle jumped in his jaw again. "Just... just say that I sent them my love."

With a flash of absolute certainty, she knew that his death would break his parents' hearts, for like the prodigal he called himself, surely he was much loved. "I'll do as you wish," she said quietly, not daring to carry the thought any further. "What will happen to the Lazy K?"

"Lord, I don't know." He rubbed his jaw, the whiskers rasping against his palm. "The Wilcoxes will keep taking care of my dog, Jenny, but I haven't wanted to think about the ranch." Abruptly he raised his head and stared at her, his gaze sharpening. "I know! I'll leave it to you."

She gasped and dropped the last hairpin. "You can't mean that. We scarcely know each other!"

He gave her a smile of great sweetness. "I'd say we know each other rather well."

She blushed again. "When you put it like that..." She retrieved the hairpin and stabbed it into the coil at the nape of her neck. "But what would I do with a ranch?"

"More than I'll be able to do," he said with bone-dry humor. "Perhaps it will let you escape the Holdens. Change your name and they'll never find you there." He began rummaging through his pockets, eventually producing a somewhat grubby piece of paper and a stub of pencil.

He was about to start writing when a thought struck

him. "Liza, would you mind if I say you're my wife? That will make it obvious why I'd leave you the Lazy K."

"Your *wife?*" she gasped. "That's unthinkable. Absurd!"

His mouth twisted. "You don't really have to be my wife, just my widow. I was away from the Lazy K long enough to fall madly in love and get married. Anyone who meets you will understand why I did."

She gave up on pinning her hair and closed her eyes as she considered. Opening her eyes again, she said reluctantly, "Claiming to be your wife—your widow—seems wrong, but it does make sense if you want to make sure the ranch goes to someone who will look out for its interests. I'll see that it's in good hands. And maybe I will need a refuge from the Holdens one day."

"Thank you, Liza! My gambler's intuition says this is the right thing to do," he said as he began writing. "What's your full maiden name?"

"Elizabeth Charlotte Baird."

He wrote that out, saying, "A good thing there isn't anyone to challenge this. Pencil on the back of a hotel bill isn't exactly correct form for a man's last will and testament."

He wrote a careful few lines, folded the paper, and wrote more, then handed it to her. "The foreman, Lou Wilcox, and his wife, Lily, will help you run the place if you decide to live there. They're good solid family people and you can trust them. The ranch hands are good people, too. They all need to be notified of my death.

I've written the names and the ranch location on the outside of this."

She accepted the paper gingerly, as if it were about to explode. She wasn't as sure as he that she would be able to elude her in-laws, but she didn't want to extinguish the light in his face. "I...I don't know what to say."

"You don't have to say anything." His brow furrowed. "Do you have any money?"

Confused, she said, "A little from my father, but Billie didn't leave much of anything. The money all belongs to his father, Big Bill. Do you need some?"

"Not unless I figure out a way to take it with me between now and Tuesday." The chain on his wrist rattled as he pulled off his right boot, then wrenched off the thick heel. Inside were gold coins packed in raw cotton to prevent clinking.

As Liza watched, bemused, he emptied out the money, replaced the heel, then repeated the process with his left boot. "I've always liked to travel with an emergency stake, in case I run into thieves or a bad run of cards," he explained as he scooped the coins up. Offering them to her, he continued, "You can use this better than I."

She stared at the gold as if it were a nest of scorpions. "I hate the idea of benefiting from your death."

"I'd like to think that someone will benefit. I sure as hell won't," he said. "I understand your scruples, Liza, but if you decide to leave the Holdens' ranch, you'll need running-away money. Matt Sloan's kangaroo court took the rest of my cash, but this is enough to take you far and fast if you want to escape."

She couldn't refuse a gesture that was clearly important to him. More than that, it was undeniable that the money might prove useful. She accepted most of the coins, but handed some back. "You may need this for bribes or food or something."

As he pocketed the gold, she added in a low voice, "Thank you, Drew. Your generosity may give me a future."

"I hope so." He gave her a light kiss. "I truly hope so."

He reclined against the flour sack again and drew her down so that she was sprawled on top of him. As he drew the blanket over her, she relaxed, content to be in his arms.

As she half-dozed, her soft weight a delicious burden, he wondered how much longer they would have.

Not long. Not nearly long enough.

SOON AFTER THE night fell ominously silent, he heard heavy footsteps approaching the storeroom. Liza inhaled sharply, then scrambled to her feet, separating them with harsh finality. Cheeks burning, she scooped up the crumpled drawers which she hadn't got around to putting on, and jammed them in a pocket. "How do I look?" she hissed as she smoothed down her skirts.

Kane rose more slowly, buttoning his trousers as he did. "Every inch a lady," he assured her, knowing it was what she wanted to hear. Brushing her cheek with the back of his knuckles, he added softly, "Also every inch a woman."

The key turned in the lock and Biff attempted to open the door, only to be blocked by the bar. "Open up!" he bellowed. "Are you all right, ma'am?"

"She's fine, Burns," Kane called. "Safer here than out there by the sound of it."

He and Liza stared at each other. The end had come

and there was too much to say to even attempt words. Fiercely, she threw her arms around his neck and gave him a bruising kiss. As he crushed her pliant body to his, he wondered despairingly how he could let her go.

Somehow he managed to do it. When his arms dropped, she stepped away, eyes bright with unshed tears as she whispered, "You will always be in my heart."

Biff roared. "Kane, if you don't open this door, I'll blow it off!"

Turning, Liza bowed her head and pressed her hands to her temples for a moment. Then she straightened and stepped forward to lift the bar. Kane retreated to the back wall, then slouched on the floor as if he had been peacefully dozing.

Accompanied by a haze of whiskey fumes, Biff entered the storeroom, his suspicious gaze going to his prisoner. "Sorry to leave you with this trash for so long, ma'am, but there was trouble and the sheriff needed me and Whittles. Did Kane bother you?"

"Not in the least," she said stiffly. "It was a most uneventful interval."

Kane made a sound that might have been a laugh that was hastily turned into a cough. Then he drawled, "Make it quick, Biff. A condemned man shouldn't have to have his sleep disturbed by a face like yours."

The deputy scowled and took a step forward, then stopped, remembering that a lady was present. Liza guessed that Drew had deliberately insulted Biff to draw attention away from her. Trying to look casual, she stooped and lifted the tray she had brought, her brain and heart numb. Already the interlude with Drew seemed incredible, dreamlike—but the warmth in his eyes was as true as anything she'd ever seen.

Biff shifted his befuddled gaze to her, and his expression changed. With heavy gallantry, he said, "Lots of purty ladies in the saloon, but none as purty as you, ma'am. Real fine hair." His hand moved vaguely, as if he was considering stroking it.

Kane's voice sliced across the room. "Biff, if you touch the little lady or upset her in any way whatsoever, I'll find a way to kill you before we reach Prairie City. I swear it."

Biff jerked, sobered by the icy menace in the prisoner's voice. "Didn't do anything," he mumbled. "Come on, ma'am, time you was away from that no-good varmint."

Liza's gaze went to Kane once more. Silently she mouthed, "I love you."

A muscle in his rigid jaw twitched. It was the last thing she saw before she turned and walked away.

Liza had thought her feelings would be too turbulent to permit sleep, but to her surprise, as soon as she went to bed she fell into a profound slumber. The next morning she awoke clear-eyed and refreshed after the best rest she'd had in years.

Her sense of well-being vanished when she remembered the events of the night before. She supposed that she should despise herself for her immorality, but she didn't. Guilt didn't have a chance compared to her searing grief at Andrew Kane's fate.

She washed and dressed mechanically, her mind going

round and round, torn between memories of Drew and the sick knowledge that he was doomed. Deciding that she felt well enough to face food, she was about to go downstairs for breakfast when she heard the soft jingle of bridles. She went to the window and saw that the skinny deputy, Whittles, had brought around three horses and Biff was leading the prisoner out of the building.

The night appeared to have helped Drew as much as Liza. No longer worn down by thirst and exhaustion, he walked tall, looking like a lord among peasants in spite of his handcuffs. As she looked down, hoping for a glimpse of his face, she remembered how he had been deprived of water during the long ride.

She would not allow it to happen again. Seizing her own canteen, which she had refilled the evening before, she dashed downstairs, across the lobby, and into the street. All three men were mounted and the party was on the verge of leaving, but she defiantly walked in front of Whittle's horse and handed the canteen to Drew. "It will be a long, dry day, Mr. Kane. I believe that you need one of these."

He inclined his head. "So I do. Thank you kindly, darlin'." Though his tone was negligent, his gaze was a caress.

Under her breath so that only Drew could hear, she said, "*Vaya con Dios*." She had often used the words, but never had she known anyone who so much needed to go with God.

Unable to bear the expression in his blue eyes, Liza turned and channeled all her anger at the situation into a furious scowl at Biff. "I trust that your journey to Prairie City will be entirely uneventful, Mr. Burns, and that your prisoner will arrive in the same condition he is now."

Even as the deputy stumblingly reassured her, she turned and went back inside. As the door closed behind her, her stomach turned sickeningly. She barely made it back to her room before she was violently ill in the chamber pot. After she lay down, hoping that her nausea would pass quickly.

Inevitably, her thoughts returned to Drew's impending execution. No honest judge or jury would have condemned a man who had killed in self-defense, but Holden money and influence were going to hang an innocent man, and there wasn't a thing Liza could do about it. Even if she got down on her knees to her father-in-law and pleaded for justice, it wouldn't help. Big Bill Holden was not a reasonable man at the best of times, and his grief and rage demanded that someone pay for the death of his son.

The problem was that Drew had not been tried by an honest judge. Federal judges were few and far between, so makeshift courts like the one Matt Sloan convened in the Gilded Rooster were common. Generally such courts did a decent job of determining guilt, but because of Matt Sloan, that hadn't happened in the case of Andrew Kane.

If a federal judge was notified, maybe he could over-rule what was clearly a miscarriage of justice. The trick would be to find a judge and persuade him to intervene soon enough to make a difference.

Liza caught her breath as she realized that Prairie City was in the same judicial district as Willow Point and Saline, and she was acquainted with the judge. Albert Barker had sometimes stopped by her father's store, and even held court there once or twice. At first she'd been surprised at Judge Barker's mild appearance, for he had a fearsome reputation for upholding the law. Then she'd looked into his implacable gray eyes, and believed everything she'd ever heard about him.

Barker wasn't just a hanging judge; he believed it was his job to free the innocent as well as to punish the guilty. If he could be reached in time and persuaded to intervene, he might be able to save Drew. A new trial, with witnesses and an honest judge, would surely acquit him. But how could she reach Judge Barker, who spent most of his time traveling and could be anywhere in his far-flung district?

Ignoring her nausea, Liza got up and wrote a letter to Judge Barker, reminding him of their past acquaintance, then relating what Drew had told her of the circumstances of Billie's shooting. After expressing a pious wish that the tragedy of her husband's death not be compounded by hanging an innocent man, she had named the two women whom Drew had mentioned. Perhaps Mei-Lin and Red Sally would have the courage to testify to what happened, even if none of the men who had been present would.

She sealed the letter and addressed it to the judge and had just scrawled URGENT across the envelope when Tom Jackson knocked. Now came the hard part.

She admitted Tom, who had a wide smile on his face. "Morning, Miz Holden. Hope you had a good night's rest. It was purely good to see my cousin Jacob and his family."

He was crossing the room to pick up her baggage when she said bluntly, "How do you feel about innocent men being hanged?"

His expression went blank and he regarded her warily. "Ma'am?"

"Something bad's going to happen, Mr. Jackson. I don't know if it can be stopped, but I want to try, and I can't do it alone." She wiped her damp palms on her skirt. "You may want to refuse, because Mr. Holden won't like what I have in mind one bit, and if he finds out, it could cost you your job."

She outlined what she had learned from Andrew Kane. Tom simply listened, his head bowed and expression inscrutable.

When she was done, he said, "You believe this Mr. Kane was telling the truth when he said it was self-defense?"

"I believed him." Her mouth twisted. "You know how Billie could be."

"I surely do. Sometimes I used to wonder how you stood..." Tom cut off his sentence.

She smiled humorlessly. "Sometimes I wondered that myself." Falling silent, she waited for his decision.

Tom gazed at his battered hat, turning it around and around in his hands. After carefully pushing out a dent in the crown, he said softly, "My brother was lynched ten years ago in Alabama because someone thought he was an uppity nigger." Raising his head, he looked Liza in the eye, his face set. "So to answer your question, no, I don't hold with hanging innocent men. What do you want me to do?"

"I've written a letter to Judge Barker," she said eagerly. "Do you think you could find out where he is now and take it to him? It will have to be done quickly. The hanging will be Tuesday in Prairie City."

Tom frowned. "I can't leave you alone."

"I'll be fine," she said. "I can stay right here in the hotel."

"Wouldn't be right," he said firmly. "Mr. Holden would have my hide for neglecting you, and rightly so."

Her eyes narrowed. "If I have to, I'll go after the judge myself."

"You can't do that, not in your condition," he said, scandalized. "Don't think I haven't noticed how tired you get riding, even slow as we've been going." He rubbed his chin, considering. "Mebbe my cousin's oldest boy, Jimmy, could go. He's smart, and a good rider."

"Then let's go ask him." Liza tied her bonnet and prepared to go downstairs. "Oh, before we leave, I'll need to stop at the general store and pick up a new canteen. I gave mine away."

Tom gave her a quizzical look that made Liza wonder if he guessed that her interest in Andrew Kane was more than an abstract desire for justice, but he said nothing. As they went outside and headed toward Tom's cousin's blacksmith shop, she gave thanks that she had confided in him.

Jacob Washington proved to be a giant of a man with a booming laugh and massive blacksmith muscles. His wife Molly laughed with equal ease, dispensing food and hugs to her active brood. Jimmy, the oldest, was a tall, slim youth of about eighteen, with steady eyes and a shy smile.

After Tom introduced Liza and said that she had something serious to discuss, she was invited into the family kitchen and the smaller children were chased away. Then, while Molly plied her with fresh cornbread and scalding coffee, Liza went through her story again.

The question of whether or not Jimmy would go was never even raised. The youth simply looked at his father and asked, "Has anyone passing through mentioned where Judge Barker is holding court now?"

Jacob rubbed his chin. "East of here, I think. Least he was a couple of weeks ago."

Molly frowned. "He'll have moved on by now, probably to the north. He usually goes that way."

After a discussion of the judge's possible whereabouts, Jimmy glanced at Liza. "I'll be on my way within the hour, ma'am."

She closed her eyes for a moment, so overcome with relief that she was almost dizzy. It was still a long shot that the execution could be stopped, but at least something was being done.

She rose and handed the letter to Jimmy, then

reached into her pocket and brought out Drew's gold. "You'll need this."

For the first time, Jacob scowled. "We don't accept money for tryin' to save a man's life."

"Of course not," she said quietly. "This isn't for your willingness, which is priceless. It's for Jimmy's expenses. There's no telling what he might run into along the way."

After a moment's hesitation, Jacob nodded and Jimmy accepted the handful of gold coins. "God bless you, Jimmy," Liza said unevenly, "and be careful traveling."

"I will be, ma'am," he said. "If Judge Barker can be found in time, I'll find him."

She prayed that he was right. After bidding the Washingtons farewell, she and Tom started back to the hotel. The excitement that came with action faded as they walked the length of Forlorn Hope's dusty main street. She had done everything in her power. Now she could do nothing but wait and see if it was enough.

It would be the easier to wrestle a cougar barehanded.

THE LAST LEG of Kane's ride was blessedly uneventful. The fury of a virtuous woman had subdued Biff and Witless. Not only did the deputies let Kane keep Liza's canteen, but they gave him some of their food. Still, it was a relief to reach their destination. Kane thought it doubtful that the deputies' improved behavior would have lasted through another day.

The Prairie City sheriff, Bart Simms, proved to be an acquaintance of Kane's. They'd met in El Paso a couple of years back, played some poker, shared a few bottles of whiskey, and told each other tall tales. Since then, Simms had grown a drooping, lugubrious mustache and acquired a tin star on his chest. In Kane's jaundiced opinion, the result was not an improvement.

Simms' shaggy brows rose when Kane was brought into the jail, but he said nothing, simply locked the prisoner in the cell in the back room. The two deputies left, with a cheerful promise to Kane that they'd come to see him on the gallows.

When they were alone, the sheriff asked, "Did you do it?"

With equal terseness, Kane said, "Self-defense."

Simms chewed his tobacco for a time. At length, he asked, "Then why're you here?"

"Because Billie Holden's uncle owned Saline, and his father owns Prairie City."

The sheriff shot a wad of tobacco juice into a spittoon. "A pity. Billie was a no-good skunk."

"I couldn't agree more." Kane regarded Simms narrowly, wondering if the sheriff's sympathy might extend to being careless enough that a prisoner might escape.

Accurately guessing Kane's thoughts, Simms said, "Sorry about this, but the law's the law."

"The law is an ass."

"Sometimes it is," the sheriff allowed. "But it's my job, and I aim to do it right." He withdrew to the front office.

Kane was unsurprised that the sheriff didn't recognize the quote; Simms wasn't the sort to spend his spare time reading Dickens. Wearily, Kane stretched out on the narrow, lumpy bunk, his hands folded beneath his head.

One of the cracks in the ceiling reminded him of the way Liza's hair fell. Actually, just about everything reminded him of her. With a faint smile, he set about recalling the time they had spent together, from the moment she had roared out of the hotel to stop the deputies from beating him to death, to the heart stopping expression in her gray eyes when they parted.

He couldn't think of a better way to spend the last four days of his life.

THE PRAIRIE CITY jail stayed boring but peaceful until the next morning. Then the door to the back room was thrown open with a force that crashed it into the wall. A heavy-set man barged in, snarling, "So this is the son of a bitch who shot my son!" Jerked out of his daydreams of Liza, it took Kane a moment to react. Big Bill Holden was broad as a barn, with a furious gleam in his small eyes and the face of a man who assumed that getting his own way was divine law. Kane felt a pang for Liza, who had lived under this man's roof for three years, and maybe would be trapped there indefinitely.

The thought made him angry. Instead of standing, Kane stayed sprawled on the bunk, as relaxed as if he were fishing on a riverbank. "So I am," he said in his most infuriating tone. "The little bastard deserved it. You should have taught him not to bully defenseless women. Better yet, you should have told him that if he was going to try to kill a man for no good reason, he should pick someone who wouldn't shoot back."

"You'll pay for that!" Holden roared with a rage that made Kane flinch involuntarily. A good thing that steel bars separated them.

As Holden reached for the Colt holstered on his hip, Kane said cordially, "Go ahead and shoot. The good citizens of Prairie City will be deprived of their show, but I'll be spared three more days of jail food. With luck, you might even be convicted of murdering an unarmed man."

After a precarious pause, Big Bill's hand dropped away from the revolver. Breathing heavily, he said, "I can't *wait* to see you swing!"

"I'm afraid you'll have to, but when the happy moment arrives, I shall try to live up to your expectations. In the meantime"—Kane pulled his black hat from under the bunk and lazily set it over his face—"leave me the bloody hell alone."

After more snarling and threats, Big Bill stormed out.

Kane exhaled slowly and laced his fingers over his midriff. He wasn't sure whether he was glad or sorry that Holden hadn't gunned him down on the spot. It would have been a quick death, better than hanging. But it was against nature to want to die, even though his prospects of survival were nonexistent.

So far, he wasn't doing badly at showing coolness in the face of death. He rather thought that the Kanes in the portrait gallery at Westlands would approve.

BY THE TIME she reached the Holden ranch, Liza was so tired that she scarcely had the energy to be depressed. At least there would a clean, quiet bed waiting for her.

After Tom Jackson helped her from her horse, she climbed the wide steps of what Big Bill boasted was the largest mansion between St. Louis and Denver. Perhaps it was; certainly it was the gaudiest.

Once inside, she removed her dusty bonnet and rubbed her aching temples. Strange to think that when she married Billie, she'd been excited at the prospect of living in such a fine place.

Alerted by the housekeeper, Adelaide came to greet her daughter-in-law. A beauty in her youth, she was still handsome. Big Bill would never have married a plain woman. "It's about time you got back." Adelaide's assessing gaze swept over Liza. "Have you been taking care of yourself?"

Liza was unsurprised that there were no questions or sympathy about her father's death. "Yes, ma'am. We rode very slowly. Mr. Jackson was most considerate."

"You need some tea as a restorative," Adelaide announced.

"Most of all, I need sleep," Liza said wearily. "If you'll excuse me..."

Adelaide raised her hand. "Very well, but before you go, I want to tell you the good news. Billie's murderer has been caught and convicted. Mr. Holden has arranged for the filthy brute to be hanged here on Tuesday."

Unable to conceal her bitterness, Liza said, "Is another death really good news? It won't bring Billie back."

"My son's death must be paid for!" Adelaide said grimly. "The Bible says an eye for an eye."

Liza's face tightened. "I hope you don't expect me to watch."

"Of course not," Adelaide said, shocked. "It might mark the baby."

Her status as brood mare firmly established, Liza excused herself and went to the bedroom she had shared with her husband. Yet, in spite of her exhaustion, she halted on the threshold, her stomach twisting.

She'd vaguely assumed that Mrs. Holden would have packed away Billie's possessions, but everything was still in place, as if he might return any minute. It was just like Adelaide to leave the bedroom as a shrine to her dead son.

Sadly, Liza leaned against the door frame, thinking of the charming young man who had courted her. The charm had been only a small part of Billie, but it had been real, and so had her love. Where had it all gone? Perhaps if she had tried harder....

Quite clearly, she heard Drew's voice in her head: *Don't blame yourself! Any man who'd treat his wife like he treated you is crazy or evil,*

His words were like a splash of cold water on the embers of her guilt. Her back straightened and she turned away. There was no point in brooding. She'd rather think Billie had been crazy, not evil. But in either case, it wasn't her fault. Moreover, she wasn't going to sleep in this room.

With a wintry smile, she headed down the corridor to the guest room. No doubt Adelaide would be happy that the shrine wouldn't be sullied by Liza's unworthy presence.

DAWN SLOWLY LIGHTENED THE CELL. Kane tried to ignore it, preferring to remain in the dream, where a soft, loving female nestled in his arms. Wheat-colored hair, unflinching gray eyes, delicious curves. He'd have enjoyed taking off Liza's garments one by one and discovering exactly what was underneath. He'd have liked waking up in his own bed at the Lazy K with her beside him. He'd have loved sitting by a fire with her while winter winds whistled off the mountains and snow piled up around the ranch house.

With a sigh, he pushed the blanket back and sat up, running his fingers through his hair. There were a hell of a lot of things he'd have liked to do that he was never going to get to. He'd always assumed that someday he'd settle down and marry, have a family. Why hadn't he done that already? Because he had never met a girl like Liza, who could be both friend and mistress, until it was too late.

He felt a piercing sorrow. With youthful arrogance he'd always assumed that eventually he'd get around to everything he wanted to do. But today, time ran out.

He drew on his boots with an odd feeling of unreality. At heart, he couldn't quite believe that he wouldn't live to see sundown. He felt too alive, too healthy.

It took only an instant for a man to die.

He looked at his hands, glad to see that they were steady. He hoped that would still be true at noon, when he was taken to the gallows.

Sheriff Simms ambled in. "Anything special you'd like for your last meal?"

Kane raised a sardonic brow. "So condemned men really do get their last request."

"If possible. What's your choice?"

"A woman?"

Amusement gleamed in the sheriff's hazel eyes. "In Prairie City, last requests only cover food, boy. The good ladies of the town wouldn't hold with such goings-on in the jail."

Kane shrugged, not having expected any other answer. It didn't matter, since Liza was the only woman he would have wanted. But it wouldn't do to waste a last request. He pondered. Unaccountably his mind leaped back to a hunt breakfast in Wiltshire. "Kippers," he announced. "I want kippers."

Simms blinked. "What the blue hell are kippers?"

"Herring that's been salted and smoked," he explained. "Delicious."

"Mebbe I can find some salted cod," the sheriff said doubtfully.

"Do your best." Kane lay back on his bunk again. "Just make sure there's a bottle of whiskey on the side."

He stared dry-eyed at the ceiling after Simms left. Three more hours.

✳

FEELING UNWELL, Liza swung her feet from the bed. As she stood, a cramp deep in her abdomen caused her to double over with pain. It passed quickly, leaving her shaky. Probably the pain was because she was so upset. She'd been hoping to hear of a miracle, but the day of Drew's execution had arrived and nothing had changed. Jimmy must not have been successful. *Ah, Drew, I did my best. I'm sorry. So sorry!*

After breakfast, Big Bill and Adelaide set off for town, identical expressions of ugly satisfaction on their faces. Liza was left alone with Janie, her sixteen-year-old sister-in-law. Since Janie had always been overlooked in favor of her brother, the two young women had become allies and friends.

The morning passed with agonized slowness as they sat in the parlor and sewed, making desultory conversation that never touched on the subject that dominated their thoughts. "It's going to be a bleak Christmas here," Janie said at one point as she sewed a black sleeve to the black bodice of a mourning gown. "I was looking forward to the holiday dance in town. My first dance." She sighed. "But that won't happen now."

Liza thought of the English Christmas that Drew had wanted to have on his Colorado ranch. Swallowing hard, she said, "No, it won't. But next year you'll be out of mourning and you can be the belle of the Christmas ball."

Janie looked wistful. At sixteen, a year seemed like

forever. She returned to her silent stitching and said no more until noon approached. Then she set her sewing aside and got restlessly to her feet. "I'm glad you didn't want to see the hanging, Liza," she confided. "Gave me an excuse not to go. I don't care if that fellow Kane did kill Billie, I couldn't have stood watching a man die."

Liza stared sightlessly at her embroidery. "On my way back from Willow Point, I heard it said that Kane killed Billie in self-defense."

Janie turned and stared at her, distressed. The girl had her mother's good looks, but a far sweeter nature. "Merciful heaven, that's dreadful if it's true!" Her voice quavered. "And Billie being Billie, it could be true, couldn't it?"

"It certainly could." As Liza stuck her needle into the fabric, a sick dizziness engulfed her and the point stabbed into her finger. Confused, she watched her blood stain the white linen with crimson. There seemed to be too much blood.

Janie said sharply, "Liza, are you all right?"

She raised her head and tried to say yes, but she couldn't make her voice work.

The mantel clock began striking with deep, melancholy tones. High noon. At this very moment, Andrew Kane was dying in agony. As the last hollow boom faded away, she closed her eyes and shuddered. *It was over*. Drew was dead.

Knowing that she should lie down, she tried to stand, but her legs wouldn't obey. She pitched to the floor, a vicious pain clenching her abdomen.

Janie's voice came from a great distance, screaming for the housekeeper. As Liza slid through the pain into darkness, she thought with anguish, *Vaya con Dios, Drew. I hope you died the kind of death you wanted. And may God have mercy on your soul.*

CHAPTER 7

SIMMS HADN'T FOUND any salted cod, so Kane's last meal was a large steak, pan-fried, with lots of gravy and a mountain of potatoes and onions on the side. Tasted a damned sight better than kippers would have.

The bottle of whiskey provided had been aged for at least a month. Prime sippin' whiskey by local standards. Nonetheless, Drew had only had a couple of shots. While the thought of drinking himself into a stupor had a certain appeal, it seemed foolish to obliterate his last minutes of life. Besides, if he was drunk, he'd be a lot more likely to lose control and disgrace himself.

The noise outside indicated that quite a crowd had gathered. There was even a brass band playing rather badly. Drew concentrated on picking out the wrong notes, preferring that to thinking the unthinkable.

All too soon Simms and a deputy with a shotgun entered the back room. The sheriff slid the key into the lock. "It's time."

Drew stood and put on his black hat, tilting it forward a little, as if he were going into a poker game with unknown opponents and wanted to look nonchalant. Then he walked out of the cell and stood still while Simms tied his hands behind his back.

Gruffly the sheriff said, "Sorry."

"You're just doing your job," Drew said tersely.

A phalanx of deputies fell in around him as he stepped outside into a harsh northern wind that whipped dust and dead leaves across the street. At least a hundred people had gathered for the show, and their shouts struck him like a bullwhip.

As his escorts forced a path through the crowd, Drew studied individual faces. Some were avid, some curious, one or two sympathetic.

Then he saw Big Bill Holden. He and Matt Sloan were standing right in front of the gallows with a well-dressed virago between them. Mrs. Holden, no doubt, and one of the few women present.

Drew inclined his head at her with mocking courtliness just to see the outrage spring into her eyes. But as he climbed the steps to the gallows, he told himself that that was not well-done. Though the woman might be a virago, she had just lost her son, and her pain was as real as anybody's. He hoped she'd be kind to Liza and Liza's child.

The crude planks of the platform creaked under his footsteps, and the death that he hadn't quite believed in became horribly real. Fear pulsed through him, making his heart hammer and his breathing turn rough. Before fear could blaze into panic, he summoned up Liza's image. Her quiet courage, her clear gray eyes that made a man feel so much a man.

He swallowed hard. He was damned well not going to die in a way that would make her ashamed of what she had given him.

The crowd was so loud that the hangman had to shout. "Any last words, Kane?"

He had to swallow again before he could reply. "Too much noise to be heard. I'm not going to die with a hoarse throat."

The hangman removed Kane's hat, then dropped the noose around his neck. The rope scratched as the noose was tightened until the knot was snug beneath his left ear. How long now? Less than a minute. *Good-bye, Liza. If there's any justice, maybe we'll meet again, when there's more time.*

He took a deep breath, trying to take his mind as far away as possible. Thank God his parents need never know how he died.

As the hangman prepared to release the trapdoor, the noise increased still further, with an ugly edge of excitement. Then a rifle fired, cutting through the din like a wire through butter.

In the startled silence that followed, a ferocious voice bellowed, "Hold it right there! This man's not for hanging!"

A babble of excitement rose, and a murmured name that sounded like Parker. Not daring to hope, Kane stared at the eddy in the crowd that was a man fighting his way toward the gallows.

When the newcomer reached the steps, he took them two at a time. He was a short, broad fellow dressed as soberly as a preacher, but he had an air of authority that didn't need the rifle he carried in one hand. Turning to face the crowd, he raised his arms and the noise died down.

"I'm Judge Barker," he boomed in a voice that could quiet the rowdiest courtroom, "and evidence has come to my attention that this man was not properly tried! That he killed Billie Holden in self-defense. I'm here to see that he goes back to Saline and gets a fair trial."

"No!" Furiously Big Bill forced his way to the steps and bounded onto the platform. "Kane's a murderer and the bastard's going to hang right now!"

Unintimidated even though he was half a head shorter, the judge retorted, "I'm the law in these parts, you son of a bitch, and I'm not going to see an innocent man hanged!"

Big Bill's hand hovered near his Colt. Then Sheriff Simms climbed onto the platform. "I wouldn't do that, Mr. Holden," he drawled. "The law's the law. If Kane's guilty, justice will be done in Saline." He glanced at Drew, and one eye closed in a slow wink.

Holden's bravado crumbled into confusion. The judge took advantage of the lull to loosen the noose around Kane's neck, then flip it over his head. "Time to make tracks, young man."

Stunned though he was by events, Kane was quick to

follow Barker off the platform and into the crowd. By sheer force of personality, the judge cleared a path as they moved away. A few disappointed citizens looked inclined to finish what had been started, but no one had the nerve to go against the judge. No one until they came across Biff Burns on the edge of the crowd.

With a growl, Biff grabbed at his former prisoner. His balance hampered by his bound hands, Kane almost fell as he twisted away from the other man's grip. "Biff," he snapped, "I've got just one thing to say to you!"

"Yeah?" Biff sneered as he tried again. "What's that?"

Kane pivoted on his left heel and swung his right foot in a ferocious kick that landed where a man least wanted it. As Biff shrieked and doubled over, Kane said coolly, "Next time you take someone to jail, show some decent manners."

The judge grabbed his arm and hustled him along. "Now that you've had your fun, boy, get your tail moving!"

Two minutes later they reached the livery stable. A slim black youth waited in front with three horses, one of them Drew's. With a flashing smile, he said, "Looks like the judge was in time, Mr. Kane!"

"Only just." Barker pulled a razor-edged Bowie knife from a sheath under his coat. "Kane, do you have enough faith in your innocence to give me your word of honor not to try to escape between here and Saline?"

"I do," he said promptly.

"You'd better keep it. Try to run away and I'll slice you into coyote bait myself." The judge circled behind

Drew and started sawing at his bonds. It didn't take long to cut through the rope and give Drew the use of his arms again. He rolled his aching shoulders, then swung onto his horse.

Barker did likewise. "Now, gentlemen, we'll be on our way before Holden forgets that he's a law-abiding man!"

They wheeled their horses and galloped out of town. After several fast miles, the judge pulled his horse back to a trot. "That should do it."

Still not quite believing that he'd escaped, Drew said, "Don't think I'm not grateful, Judge Barker, but how the devil did you happen to show up at such a propitious moment?"

"You have a young lady to thank for that. Billie Holden's widow had Jimmy here bring me a letter. I figured if the dead man's widow thought you might be innocent, the situation was deserving of my attention."

My God, Liza had done it! Kane thought, amazed. Not only had she given him the happiest hours he'd ever known, but she'd saved his life. *Oh, Liza, sweet Liza, will I be able to save you from your captivity?*

He thought of her sharing a house with Big Bill Holden and the virago, and scowled. When he was cleared of the murder charge, he'd look into that. If she wanted to run away, he'd see that she made her escape safely.

Touching his heels to his horse, he said, "Onward to Saline, gentlemen. The sooner we get this over with, the better!"

✳

LIZA REMEMBERED MERCIFULLY few of her nightmares. She knew that Janie was sometimes with her, and other shadowy forms, but when she finally returned to full consciousness, Adelaide was the woman sitting by the bed.

Her voice a thread, Liza asked, "The man who killed Billie. They hanged him?"

Adelaide swallowed hard, a strange expression on her face, before she said stiffly, "Yes."

Liza closed her eyes and tears spilled from under her lids. "I...I lost the baby, didn't I?"

"You did," Adelaide said, not trying to conceal her bitterness. "But the doctor said you would be fine, and there was no reason why you couldn't have children in the future."

"I'm sorry," Liza whispered. She felt empty, too hollow even to grieve.

"So am I." Adelaide stood and gazed at her with hooded eyes. "He should have married a woman who was stronger."

Once again, it was all Liza's fault. Her voice choked, she said, "As soon as I'm able, I'll leave the ranch."

"As Billie's widow, you're entitled to live here as long as you want." Her mother-in-law said flatly.

Adelaide would always do her duty, no matter how little she liked it. "You're very generous," Liza said wearily, "but I think it would be best for everyone if I left."

"Yes. It would."

As her mother-in-law turned to leave, Liza said, "You've had two great losses, and I truly grieve for you. But don't forget that you have another child, and she needs you."

Adelaide stopped short. Then, after a half dozen heartbeats, she gave an infinitesimal nod.

Alone again, Liza turned her face into the pillow and let the tears come. She had the freedom she had craved, but at such a price! It was the freedom of absolute aloneness. *Oh, Drew, if only you could be here for five minutes, to hold me in your arms and tell me that someday things would be better than they are now.*

She couldn't have him, but she could go to the home that he had loved. There, perhaps, she could find a measure of peace.

LIZA PROBABLY SHOULD HAVE RESTED LONGER after her miscarriage, but the atmosphere at the Holden ranch was unbearable. Neither a wife nor mother, she had no place there, so she left as soon as her strength started to come back. Apart from Adelaide's token offer of a home, no one tried to prevent her from leaving, though Janie shed heartfelt tears.

Just before departing, Liza said a quick good-bye to Tom Jackson. Neither of them referred to the futile attempt to save Andrew Kane. She couldn't have borne it.

The only possessions she took away from her marriage to a rich man's son were the fine mare that had been Billie's present their first Christmas, and as much clothing as would fit into her saddlebags. Dressed like a man, Elizabeth Charlotte Baird Holden, unsuitable wife, failed brood mare, unfortunate reminder, vanished from the Triple H ranch as if she had never set foot there.

In spite of her fatigue and the emptiness inside her, Liza's bleakness began to lift as she rode north. Though she still wasn't sure she could accept Drew's legacy of the ranch, she looked forward to seeing his home. There she would write the letter to his parents that she'd promised to send.

Mentally she tried to figure out what to say, and the task was proving as hard for her as it had been for Drew. How should she start? *Dear Sir Geoffrey and Lady Kane, your son is dead. He was a gambler and maybe a bit of a rogue, and the kindest man I ever met. He left a ranch he loved. It should go to you, but since you probably won't come to Colorado, maybe I'll keep it myself and try to run it as he would have liked.*

With a sigh, she set the project aside. She'd worry about it when she got to Colorado.

Even though Liza had been pretty sure that her fast, grain-fed mare could outrun trouble, luckily she didn't have to prove it. She took the long ride in easy stages, and by the time she reached Pueblo, she was almost her old self, at least physically. An inquiry at the general store gave her directions to the Lazy K, and she headed up into the hills.

When she reached the top of the last ridge and gazed down into the valley, she saw that Drew had told the truth: it really was the most beautiful place on God's earth, with spectacular mountains above and greenery marking the path of a swift creek. So this was the place that had changed Drew from a ramblin', gamblin' man into a landowner like his stuffy ancestors.

She smiled. Maybe some of those ancestral Kanes were less respectable than they had appeared in their portraits. She'd like to think so.

She rode into the valley slowly, feeling as if she was completing a pilgrimage. The long, low ranch house was built of thick-walled adobe so it would be cool in the summer and stand firm against the winds of winter.

As she approached, she saw a stocky middle-aged man coming from a smaller building to the left. A dog ambled at his side. Guessing that it was the foreman, Lou Wilcox, and the dog might be Jenny, she squared her shoulders and trotted toward the man and dog.

She was Eliza Kane now, and she had bad news to deliver.

KANE'S second trial at the Gilded Rooster lasted considerably longer than the first. Led by Red Sally and the halting, accented words of Mei-Lin, the parade of witnesses attesting to his innocence was a long one. Cynically, Kane ascribed the testimony of the men to the fact that Matt Sloan was still out of town. The women, he guessed, would have testified at the first trial if they'd been allowed to.

After the last witness had spoken, Judge Barker banged his gavel on the bar. "A clear case of self-defense. Mr. Kane, you are acquitted of all charges!"

Kane checked the coins in his pocket, calculating how much he'd need to get back to Colorado. A good thing Liza had suggested he keep some of the money. Taking out what he could spare, he slapped the gold coins on the bar. "Ladies and gentlemen, in honor of the fact that justice has been served, the drinks are on me until this runs out!"

A cheer went up. The saloon owner, the very man who had presided over the first trial, shrugged and started setting out bottles and glasses. Business was business.

Drew picked up a bottle and two glasses and made his way to the judge. "Thanks again, Judge Barker. You're a credit to the federal judiciary." He poured two drinks and handed one over.

Being off duty, Barker beamed and accepted the whiskey. "A pleasure, my boy. I never could stand Matt Sloan or Big Bill Holden. The bastards think they're above the law." He raised the glass and drained it in one swallow. "And I got a bonus out of your case. That Jimmy's a clever lad. He's going to be my clerk and read law with me."

"Excellent!" Drew emptied his glass, then set it on the bar. "Give him my best wishes. Now I'm going home."

The judge peered over his spectacles. "I suggest that if you're riding north, you give Prairie City a wide berth."

Drew nodded, having come to the same conclusion. He'd have to wait until he got back to the Lazy K before trying to find out how Liza was. He'd send someone to make discreet inquiries, since showing his own face in Prairie City would be distinctly unhealthy, and not just for him. It wouldn't do for Liza to be seen communicating with him, and the last thing he wanted was to cause her trouble.

As he collected his horse at the livery stable, he gave serious thought to the question of what it would be like to raise Billie Holden's child. Liza would be the mother, so the kid couldn't be all bad. Likely Kane and Liza would have children, too. He hoped so; his close brush with death made him want a family as he never had before.

How long would it take to reach the Lazy K? If he was lucky and no blizzards blasted in from the plains, he could make it home for Christmas. There wouldn't be time to organize the English celebration he'd wanted, but at least he'd be *home*.

A smile on his face, he turned his horse north and set out on the long ride.

WINTER CAME EARLIER in the mountains and Liza had already seen light snowfalls at the Lazy K. When she tossed and turned at night, cold winds rattled the tree outside her window. But the ranch house had been built well and it kept her warm and safe.

A soft, comforting whimper came from the other side of the bed, and Liza smiled as she stroked Jenny's sleek head. Drew's dog had accepted her as an adequate substitute for her master, and had explained in doggie sign language that she expected to sleep on the bed. She was good company on the long nights.

Liza had swiftly fallen in love with the Lazy K and everyone who lived on the ranch. Even though she'd never seen Drew here, his books and clothes and occasionally whimsical possessions created a vivid sense of his personality. Sometimes she felt as if he was just around the corner and if she moved fast enough, she'd catch up with him.

It was all too easy to imagine him in his bed, though. Jenny was a good dog, but she was no substitute for Drew. That's why Liza was having trouble sleeping.

Strange how a man whom she had known for such a short time could have imprinted her soul so thoroughly. She wondered whether the tragic circumstances of his death meant that he would become a ghost and haunt the living. If so, his ghost would be welcome here any time.

She'd told Lou and Lily Wilcox that she and Drew had fallen in love and married right away, and he'd died defending her from a couple of bandits. The story had a core of truth since his death was the result of protecting an innocent young girl, and Liza wanted Drew remembered as the hero he was. The Wilcoxes had never questioned her story. As soon as he saw the crude will on the back of the hotel bill, Lou said that he'd recognize that fancy English handwriting anywhere.

As Drew had promised, Lou and Lily did everything they could to help her learn about the ranch. The Lazy K was a well-run spread, larger and more prosperous than she had expected. His parents would have been impressed if they'd ever visited.

A thought struck her. Drew wouldn't be here, but in his honor, she'd give the Lazy K the Christmas he'd wanted. She'd ask Lou Wilcox to cut a blue spruce tree for the parlor. The general store in town was a good one, and she'd buy colored paper and ribbons and bright calico fabric to make decorations. Then she'd bake gingerbread cookies just like she and her mother used to do. She'd cut them into stars and hang then high enough on the tree that Jenny couldn't reach them.

One of the ranch hands, Miguel, liked carving small figures for his two little girls. She'd commission him to make some ornaments for the tree. And a crèche! She'd love to have a Nativity scene under the branches of the tree.

Another thought struck. She'd found Drew's strong box, and the Lazy K could well afford to put candles in every window, like he'd described at his parents' house. She'd get tin lanterns to reflect the light out and cut the risk of fire.

Then she'd have a Christmas dinner for everyone on the ranch. The Wilcoxes, the cook and her husband, all the ranch hands and the nearest neighbors as well. She'd provide most of the food, but anyone who wanted to could bring a dish in neighborly Western style. Tamales were a traditional Mexican holiday treat, and those made by Miguel's wife, Anita, were delicious. Liza would ask if she could bring a batch.

It wouldn't be like a fancy feast at Westlands, Drew's family home, but it would be friendly and welcoming, and maybe the candles in the windows would call Drew's spirit home. And at the height of the feast, she'd make a toast to his memory.

Smiling and spinning plans, she draped an arm over Jenny and drifted into peaceful sleep

LIZA'S CHRISTMAS plans were greeted enthusiastically by everyone on the ranch, and preparations kept her so busy that she was tired enough to sleep. By Christmas Eve, the Lazy K was ready to celebrate in its own mixture of English and American Christmas. Everyone invited volunteered to bring a dish, and there would be fiddling and dancing after the meal.

But on this night before Christmas, Liza was alone and even having Jenny beside her didn't help her fall to sleep. After a couple of hours of tossing and turning, she sighed and swung her feet from the bed to the brightly woven Indian rug that warmed the floor. She'd promised to write Drew's parents, and she might as well do it tonight since she was already in a weepy mood.

It was too chilly to walk around in her flannel nightgown, so she donned a robe of Drew's. The garment was black velvet with flamboyant scarlet and gold trim, exactly what she would have expected a successful gambler to wear. Though she suspected that it was not entirely wise to take such pleasure in wearing his clothing, she loved the feel of the robe, and the faint, masculine scent that was uniquely his.

Sadly she slipped on a pair of warm wool socks, then padded into the parlor to write the most difficult letter of her life.

A SMART MAN would have spent the night in Pueblo, but then, a smart man would have stayed in England and become a solicitor. Kane pushed on through the night, unwilling to stop when it was Christmas Eve and he was so close to home. There would be time enough to rest when he and his horse reached the Lazy K.

He started to have second thoughts when snow began to fall. First it was only light, dry flakes, but the closer he came to his valley, the heavier the snow fell and the more bitter the winds. As he started the final stretch down toward the ranch, he slowed his tired horse to a walk, afraid he'd miss the house as the visibility dropped to near zero. On a night this cold, getting lost could be fatal for both of them.

He was beginning to curse himself for not stopping in Pueblo when he saw dim lights ahead. What the...? Maybe the Wilcox house. He hadn't thought he'd ridden that far, but it was impossible to be sure.

No, not the Wilcoxes, but his own house! The half dozen windows facing the road all had candles glowing behind the glass, shining through the blowing snow to guide him home. He caught his breath, startled by the sight. He must have mentioned the candles to the Wilcoxes and Lily Wilcox decided to light the candles in honor of the English Christmas he'd hoped for.

Numb with fatigue, he took his exhausted horse into the stables and rubbed the stalwart beast down and fed it generously. Then he crossed the yard to the house, drawn by the golden glow of the candles. They were set in sturdy tin lanterns for safety's sake, and they burned a welcome for travelers. He swallowed hard as he thought of his mother and Westlands.

The front door was unlocked, which didn't surprise him, but the warmth, the tangy scent of fresh spruce, and the glow of lights did. Since the Wilcoxes had their own house, his place should be empty. Unless someone was staying here to light the candles at nightfall and put them out in the morning?

He'd barely closed the door behind him when he heard a scrabble of claws and Jenny bolted toward him from the parlor that ran across the back of the house, a smile of doggy bliss on her furry face. He knelt and hugged her. "Good girl!" he murmured into her glossy neck, glad that someone was here to welcome him home. She wriggled enthusiastically and licked his face with welcome warmth.

Not wanting to fall asleep in the middle of the entry way, he stood and peeled his heavy, sodden riding coat off and removed his boots. After hanging his coat on one of the hall pegs, he padded toward the light in the parlor. He could see that a low, steady fire was burning in the fireplace and filling the rooms with blessed warmth.

When he reached the parlor, he stopped in the door-way, amazed. Not only was there a fire, but a fragrant Christmas tree stood in the right-hand corner, the tin star on top almost scraping the ceiling. There were ribbon chains and ornaments, and gingerbread scented the air along with the fresh tang of the blue spruce.

He realized that not all the light came the fire and glanced to the right. Someone was working at his desk.

He caught his breath at the sight of the small figure, sure his imagination was betraying him because he'd thought of Liza so often.

But he'd never thought of putting her in his own black velvet robe, which fit her slim frame like socks on a rooster. "Liza?" he asked incredulously.

His shock was nothing compared to hers. She had been frowning over a letter, her expression intent, but she glanced up at the sound of his voice.

With a horrified gasp, she dropped her pen, black ink spraying across the paper. Her face went dead white.

They stared at each other for what seemed like forever. In his dreams, Drew had assumed that if they met again, they would go straight into each other's arms. Instead, he was painfully aware that in many ways they were strangers.

With a crooked smile, he said, "I know that I've been wearing the same clothes for the last few weeks, but surely I don't look that frightening."

Disbelieving, she stood and walked slowly toward him, the hem of his robe trailing across the carpet. "Drew," she whispered. "Is it really you? Not a ghost?"

He began to laugh, and as soon as she came within reach he caught her in his arms and pulled her close. "What do you think?"

She began shaking. "M-Mrs. Holden said that you had been hanged!"

With a happy sigh, Drew leaned against the door frame and rested his chin on her head. She felt even better than he remembered, probably because she was wearing a lot less. "The lady should have known better. She had a front row view when Judge Barker stomped up and said he was taking me back to Saline for a new trial."

Liza's head shot up, her gray eyes wide. "Then it worked? Jimmy Washington found the judge in time?"

"That he did, though he and the judge cut it pretty close." Drew made a rueful face. "Two minutes longer would have been too late. Scared me out of five years' growth."

"Mrs. Holden looked odd when I asked her if the execution had taken place. She must have assumed that I wanted Billie's killer dead, and since I was ill, she told me what she thought I wanted to hear. Probably the one and only time she tried to be considerate. When I said goodbye to Tom Jackson, he must have thought I knew what had really happened." Liza gave a choked giggle. "I was sitting here trying to write the letter to your parents that you asked me to send. Lucky I was so slow!"

"I'm glad to hear that," he said wholeheartedly. "But you say you were ill?" With a frown, he put his hands on her shoulders and studied her critically. "You do look a bit peaked. What happened?"

Her gaze dropped to the limp ruffles of his shirt. "I— I lost the baby."

He wrapped his arms around her again and began rocking her gently. "Oh, Liza, sweetheart! You lost so much, so quickly! That must have hurt dreadfully even though you hated the prospect of having to stay with the Holdens."

As Jenny twined around them both, Liza began to cry,

his sympathy causing all of her sorrows of the last weeks to pour out uncontrollably. Only when her tears began to subside did she realize the strangeness of the situation. Breaking away from his embrace, she said shyly, "It must look odd to you, me acting as if I own the place."

He smiled and took off his hat and skimmed it onto a chair with a flick of the wrist. "Well, you thought you did. That robe looks better on you than it ever did on me."

Self-consciously she drew the velvet panels together to cover her nightgown. "I'll get out of your way tomorrow."

He straightened, his humor dropping away. "Why would you do a silly thing like that? Especially on Christmas! Where would you go? Much more sensible for you to stay here, particularly since you came as my widow." His voice softened. "I surely would like it if you do stay. Time I married and settled down and became respectable. Will you marry me, Eliza?"

Her mouth dropped open. "How can you talk about marriage? We hardly know each other! My husband has been dead only a few weeks!"

"And I killed him," Drew said flatly. "Is that an impassable obstacle?"

"I'm not blaming you for that," she said in a frantic bid for sense. "But there's plenty of other reasons not to marry!"

"Such as?" He studied her face, his expression sardonic. "I think I understand. It was one thing to have a quick tumble when we were strangers in the night, both feeling desperate and lonesome, but that doesn't mean I'm good husband material. Mad, bad, and dangerous to know. A lady smart as you could certainly do better."

"You've got it backward!" she said, outraged. "You're a rich, handsome man with a ranch and a fancy pedigree. What would you want with a penniless widow whom you've only known for a few hours?" She blushed furiously. "A woman who behaved in a manner that must have given you an extremely low opinion of her morals!"

His tension eased and he smiled, with devastating effect. "The way you behaved gave me an extremely *high* opinion of you. You're brave, lovely, and kind, and you saved my life." He reached out and began playing with her hair. "You're a dangerous woman, Liza. Not only have you got me roped and tied, but I can't wait to be branded."

She shivered as he stroked the curve of her ear. "You don't have to marry me because you're grateful for what I did, or because you feel guilty about shooting Billie."

"Neither guilt nor gratitude come into it." With his dark tousled hair and rogue's charm, he looked like every mother's nightmare, and every girl's dream. "Besides the fact that you're the most wonderful woman I've ever met, it would be downright humiliating to miraculously return from the dead and have my grieving widow hightail out of here the next day!"

"I can say that we hadn't actually married and once we met up again, we decided we wouldn't suit each other," she suggested. "You called me your wife in your will just so it would be clear why I was your heir. That's mostly true."

He shook his head. "Too complicated. Much easier to find a parson and make it legal." He smiled as he glanced around the warm, welcoming room. "You've given me the home I wanted for Christmas, Liza. But what makes it perfect is my Christmas angel, and that's you."

She glared at him. "Just because we helped each other when we were at the end of our tethers doesn't mean there should be anything more between us!"

His fingers skimmed down her throat, warm and sensual. "Is that all that was between us, Liza, a little shared comfort in the midst of misery?"

Why did his delicious English accent have to make her bones feel like butter? Her pulse was pounding and she was having trouble thinking. "It...it meant a lot more than that to me."

"It was more than just a night to me, too," he said pensively. "I think I would have fallen in love with you under any circumstances, but since we had so little time, it happened in an instant. To me, it felt as if we skipped right over the usual courtship and went directly heart to heart."

His hand curved behind her neck and a gentle pressure urged her closer. "We've both suffered some terrible things in the last few weeks, Liza. You lost a husband, a father, a child. I killed a man, which I hoped I'd never have to do, and I almost died on the scaffold." He tilted her chin up. "The only good thing that happened was meeting you. Don't we have an obligation to take that seed of goodness and help it grow into something that's even better?" He bent his head and touched his lips to hers.

His kiss was everything she remembered and more, a promise of both passion and protection. She leaned into his embrace, loving the feel of his warm, muscular body. "Oh, Drew, I'm not very good at being noble!" she whispered. "If you aren't careful, you'll be stuck with me for life."

He gave a gusty sigh of satisfaction. "Now there's a life sentence I can live with! I wonder how long it will take to find a parson? I want to get a ring on your finger before you change your mind."

"I decided to have a grand Christmas feast tomorrow in your honor," she said hesitantly. "Well, not a grand feast, but a friendly Western one. Pastor Swenson is going to be one of the guests and he'll hold a short service before the meal."

Drew gave a whoop of laughter. "Perfect! We'll say we wanted to make our vows again in front of all our friends. No one need know it's our real marriage ceremony." He bent to give her another lingering kiss. "Are you willing, my lovely Liza?"

In a flash of pure knowing, the last of Liza's doubts vanished. Maybe they had started their relationship in the middle rather than the beginning, but that didn't mean their feelings weren't real. This was *right,* and she'd never been more sure of anything in her life. "I'm willing, Drew," she breathed. "You're my Christmas miracle and I'd be a fool to let you get away!"

"As long as you'll have me, I'm not going anywhere," he said softly. "Now what will we tell people to explain why I'm not dead?"

She thought. "I told everyone here that you saved me from two robbers who wanted to kill us. How about if I say as you were fighting them off, you told me to ride off as fast as I could. Being an obedient wife, naturally I did that. As I escaped, I heard gunshots and one of the robbers said you were dead."

"And he was wrong. I was wounded and it took time to recover, but I'm home again just in time for Christmas," Drew said cheerfully as he circled her shoulders with one arm. "Now that that's settled, I would dearly like to go to bed." He cocked a mischievous eye at her. "Preferably with you."

When she halted in mid-stride, he said hastily, "Just to sleep. I imagine that after what happened, you're not ready for anything more." His voice became intense. "But, Lord, I'd like so much to spend the night with you in my arms, and wake up and find you there."

"I'd like that, too." She grinned. "I hope you don't mind having Jenny on the bed with us."

He laughed. "She's a very persuasive dog, isn't she?"

"Indeed she is." Liza slipped her arms around his neck. "Did I mention that I love you?"

For a suspended moment, there was silence. Then he said quietly, "The feeling is entirely mutual, my darling girl."

This time she started the kissing, losing track of time and place in a rush of joyous emotion. Vaguely she became aware that they were wrapped around each other like squash vines, her back was flat against the wall of the corridor, and the velvet robe had fallen around their feet.

Lifting his head, he said hoarsely, "We're not making much progress toward that bedroom!"

She laughed and started unbuttoning his dilapidated shirt. "I'm feeling fit as a fiddle. We can see how it goes. Of course, if you're too tired..." Her voice trailed off provocatively.

"Not that tired!" He swooped her up in his arms and carried her, laughing, to the bedroom as Jenny trotted behind them. After he deposited Liza gently on the bed, he bent over her, his arms braced on either side of her head. "A good thing you didn't manage that letter to my parents. Now when I write, it will be good news instead of bad." He kissed the tip of her nose.

She slid her arms around his neck and pulled him down beside her. "The best news, my dangerous man. The very best!"

AUTHOR'S NOTE

THANK you for taking the time to read *Christmas Candles*. I hope you've enjoyed it—and if so, please consider helping other readers find it by leaving a review of the novel at your favorite online bookstore or reader website.

The Best Husband Money Can Buy is now also available as an audiobook, narrated by Siobhan Waring.

If you'd like to read more holiday tales, look for my *Christmas Revels,* which contains five Christmas novellas, four historical and one contemporary; some of those novellas are also available as individual ebooks: *The Black Beast of Belleterre, Sunshine for Christmas, The Christmas Cuckoo,* and *A Holiday Fling.*

I also have stories in holiday anthologies: *Seduction on a Snowy Night, A Yuletide Kiss, Christmas Roses* (along with Patricia Rice and Susan King), and two Kensington anthologies done with all eight Word Wenches: *The Last Chance Christmas Ball* and *Mischief and Mistletoe.*

Finally, if you would like me to let you know when my upcoming books are published, you can join my newsletter at MaryJoPutney.com.

Happy reading!
Mary Jo Putney

Uncommon Vows

The Rake

The Bargain

The Marriage Spell (paranormal)

Putney Classics (Sweet Regency Romances)

Carousel of Hearts

The Diabolical Baron

The Lackland Abbey Chronicles

(Young Adult fiction, written as M. J. Putney)

Dark Mirror, #1 (includes a bonus Lackland short story)

Dark Passage, #2

Dark Destiny, #3

The Guardian Trilogy

(Historical fantasy, written as M.J. Putney)

A Kiss of Fate, #1

Stolen Magic, #2

A Distant Magic, #3

The Lost Lords Series

Loving A Lost Lord, #1

Never Less Than A Lady, #2

Nowhere Near Respectable, #3

No Longer A Gentleman, #4

Sometimes A Rogue, #5

Not Quite A Wife, #6

Not Always a Saint, #7

Rogues Redeemed Series (A Spin-Off of the Lost Lords)

Once A Soldier, #1

Once a Rebel, #2

Once A Scoundrel, #3

Once A Spy, #4

Once Dishonored, #5

Once A Laird, #6

The Circle of Friends Trilogy

The Burning Point, #1

The Spiral Path, #2

An Imperfect Process, #3

A Holiday Fling (novella, also published in Christmas Revels)

Shorter Works

Weddings of the Century: A Pair of Novellas

The Best Husband Money Can Buy (novella, also published in Christman Candles)

The Christmas Cuckoo (novella, also published in Christmas Revels)

The Black Beast of Belleterre (novella, also published in Christmas Revels)

Sunshine for Christmas (novella, also published in Christmas Revels)

The Dragon and the Dark Knight (written as M.J. Putney)

Christmas Collections

Christmas Revels

Christmas Candles

Mischief and Mistletoe (contributor)

The Last Chance Christmas Ball (contributor)

Christmas Roses (contributor)

Seduction on a Snowy Night (contributor)

A Yuletide Kiss (contributor)

ABOUT THE AUTHOR

A *New York Times, Wall Street Journal,* and *USAToday* best-selling author, Mary Jo Putney is also a recipient of RWA's Nora Roberts Lifetime Achievement Award. She was born in Upstate New York with a reading addiction, a condition for which there is no known cure. Her entire romance writing career is an accidental byproduct of buying a computer for other purposes.

Her novels are known for psychological depth and intensity and include historical and contemporary romance, fantasy, and young adult fantasy. Winner of numerous writing awards, including two RITAs and two *Romantic Times* Career Achievement awards, she's had a number of her books listed as top romances of the year by *Library Journal* and *Booklist,* the magazine of the American Library Association.

Her favorite reading is great stories, but in a pinch she'll settle for the backs of cereal boxes. She's delighted that e-publishing can now make available books that have been out of print.

Manufactured by Amazon.ca
Bolton, ON